An Older Wine

A Collection of
Notes, Letters, and Short
Stories from a Southern
Woman's Suitcase

by Patsy Stanley

ISBN-978-1- 7328552-5-0

Library of Congress Control Number 2015908432

Table of Contents

This book is dedicated to Mom and Lois, two of Heaven's best berry pickers. "Come on girls, it's berry pickin' time agin'!"

1.   **Blackberry Beach**

Dear folks,

It's been a long time, and I hope you're all a' farin' well... I thought I'd better take up paper and pen and write a letter to go along with the little somethin' I'm a' sending ye'.

You all remember Arnie, don't ye'? What a time we've had, a' livin' in this faraway place up on the edge of the world? There's jist' me and him here in the middle of this big old fast city.

These mountains stay cold, and the rain falls never ending. They're not like the mountains and sunlight back home. The houses press right up against each other. The people drive by so fast you cain't even study their faces ta' see what kind of day they're a' havin', or tell who they are.

It's very noisy here. Hard to hear yourself think. If you're a' havin' strong thoughts ye' need ta' ponder awhile, this ain't the place fer' it.

There ain't a level foot of ground to be found anywhere, either. The house we live in sets in the side of a hill. When I look out one winda', the neighbor woman is a' lookin' down on me through her winda'. When I look out the winda' on the other side of the house, I'm a' lookin' down on the woman that lives below me.

Arnie's gone most of the time, a' drivin' all over, sellin' them furnaces to people. I never know when he's gonna' be home. He's like a race car driver out there. Knows exactly where ever' place is and just how to git' there fast. He likes goin' ever' where and laughin' and talkin' it up

1

with folks. That's why he's salesman of the month all the time. When he gets home, he never fails to laugh real big and pick me up and twirl me in circles 'til I'm half dizzy. Arnie always says that just because there's snow on the roof don't mean there ain't no fire in the furnace. Men.

I know you're all a' wonderin' about the kids. They're doin' fine. I call em' pretty often and get the grandbabies on the phone and talk to 'em and send 'em pictures of the little garden I've growed out back of the house. I got their pictures all over the 'frigerator.

Remember Aunt Shelby Poem allus' talkin' to her green beans? She talked to 'em the whole time they was a' growin' up. Ever' time she went to the garden, she'd talk to them beans. She made em' pretty when she canned em' up, too. Wasn't nobody else to talk to, I guess, so they was her company. She scolded em' and laughed with em' and went on. Me and her's jist' a little bit alike that way. Only she stayed up in the hills back home, and I moved here.

Old Arnie likes this place. He plays basketball with a bunch of men ever' week. When they ain't playin', they're a' watchin' sports together.

When Arnie's home, he's like a hen on a hot rock. He cain't set still fer' five minutes unless he's in front of the television. He watches them sports announcers like they're tent revival preachers, and he's ready ta' git' saved. He knows ever' thing about ever player. I told him he was real good with sports talk, and he said he should a' been a sports announcer on the radio. I used to try to get him to set with me and talk about things around the house, but he likes whatever he sees on that television better.

Well, after bein' here awhile and cleanin' up around this place, I got so I was runnin' in circles. A body cain't step out and find a quiet place to rest like we could back home. I was a' doin' the same thing over and over. I knowed that wouldn't do me no good, so I got to thinkin' I better chaince' gettin' out and seein' some more of what there is to see in this big old scary place, sa' loud and fast and stinkin' like old Mrs. Dutton's hound dog that liked ta' eat possum.

I stayed quiet and give old Arnie some long, sad looks. I did it that a' way, cause he's dense as a door knob. I noticed that about that batch of men he runs with, too. Well, it took him awhile to catch on, but he finally did.

Last Sunday mornin', bright and early, he was up and in the kitchen before I got out of bed. He set there, a' drinkin' that old strong coffee he makes that's thick as mud. I don't drink coffee no more cause' if I do, it makes my heart pound like a horse jumpin' a high fence. He fixed breakfast instead of me a' doin' it. I waited to hear what was on his mind, and I knowed what it better be. After a while, he rared back in his chair and looked at me.

"Why don't we take the ferry someplace today?"

I went wild. I jumped up and danced a jig. He knows I'm like a little kid when I get on them ferries. Never seen nothin' like em'. They're big and open with fresh air a' blowin' over ye', and life jackets, so you don't need to know how to swim 'cause I cain't.

We got ready and took off. Arnie parked the car and we walked onto the ferry. We rode it across to an island and got off. Arnie was a' grinnin' at me and eatin' popcorn. I never seen such a one fer' eatin' all the time.

We went down white painted stairs and out on the beach.

"Look over there!" Arnie said. He pointed to a yella' cliff about thirty feet high. There was the biggest bunch of thick blackberry vines runnin' right down that cliff to the sand you ever saw. Every vine was loaded with blackberries as big as Arnie's thumb. And Arnie has big old hands. I could see the berries was dead ripe and dark and juicy. I asked Arnie why them berries hadn't been picked, and he told me the oddest thing. He said the people here don't think nothin' of em'. They grow wild all over the place, and people won't even pick em', while we'd go crazy to have em' back home.

Well, I run over to em' and stood in the sand lookin' em' over. I felt the ocean air comin' off a' that water running over me and them berries. I sniffed the tangy salt smell and felt the water in that wet air, and I thought about what it would be like to be one a' them berries doin' nothin' but hangin' there with the sun and watery air a' washin' over me all day.

I picked a berry and popped it in my mouth, and I'm a tellin' you, the world lit up like it used to in our little church back home! That old sun kept a' shinin' down. I took Arnie's popcorn bag away from him and went to pickin' blackberries.

Arnie knows I carry a gallon plastic bag in my purse with a stomach seltzer and a wet wash cloth in it in case I get a hot flash. I dumped them right out on the ground and filled it up, too.

Arnie was a' laughin' and a' helpin' me, and we was both eatin' berries as hard as we could, with people a' walkin' up and down that beach a' starin' at us like we was nuts, and me not one bit bashful for once. They was the sweetest berries I believe I ever tasted!

When I got done, I set down on a log, and started thinking about me a' bein' in this place a' pickin' blackberries in the sand in my bare feet. Pickin' em' while the warm sun was a' shinin' by the ocean a few feet away in a land I never knew was on Earth.

A cool, magic, gray land heavy with water and rocks. I listened ta' the voices of the little waves tossing themselves up on the beach before they run back out, and I knowed God give me Heaven on Earth in this place, on this very day.

I thought about Mom and Lois and all of you, scattered ever where and sa' far away. I thought about my dear children and my tall, graceful mother. We picked wild strawberries together when I was young, in sandy fields where they was skimpy and few, but worth the hunt, for they tasted so good. Remember us a' pourin' thin curls of hot maple syrup in the snow and eatin' it like candy when it hardened, and laughin' and runnin' here and there like wild things without a care?

Remember Darnell and Pearly runnin' to the back of the church up in the holler back home, and thowin' the doors wide open so the wind could carry away the shoutin' out into nature?

I guess the shoutin' was too big to be closed up in any one place, and on that beach I knowed why.

I yearned right then to have every one of you'ns I have cherished all of my life to be there with me on that beach. I wanted all of us to pick blackberries together and laugh and set on that old bleached log out in the sun. I wanted ever body to plant their bare feet in that white sand, and look out over that ocean with them blackberries a' hangin' down that rock cliff a few feet behind us. I wanted you'ns to witness with me, but all I had on that beach was Arnie and God.

I picked a few more berries. When I'd filled up everything I could find with them, I set em' down and hugged Arnie like he was never hugged by me before. We started for home, and I carried them blackberries like they was precious jewels.

When we got there, I carried em' in the house and set ta' sortin' and cleanin' em' as fast as I could. I got my best little fancy jars out of the pantry, warshed em' up good and got em' ready. Then I boiled them berries down into the prettiest jam you ever seen.

I sung songs of praise over them while I stirred, and their good smellin' steam rose up over me. I sung songs for Mom and Pop and my sisters and ever' body else that crossed my mind. I ain't no good at singin', but I didn't let that stop me. I sung "Amazin' Grace," and the rubber duckie song I sang to my kids when they was little and so sweet, a' playin' in the bath tub. I give "Paradise" a good try, and fell down on "Blue Suede Shoes," but got back up again on "I'll Fly Away."

Arnie set in his recliner watching television in the other room. Ever little while he come in the kitchen and grinned and shook his head. He laughed and said I was makin' such a big racket he could barely hear the television.

When I got done, there was a pretty good batch of filled jars a' settin' there coolin' off, lookin' like the darkest purple jewels in little jars. Every jar with them berries in it was full of the sound that water made washin' up close to em' while they was a' growin' up and a' fillin' out. They was full of the songs I sung to 'em and all a' that good feelin' that rose up in me. The salty tang of that wet sea air was in em' and the warm sunshine that made em' drowsy so they could just hang there and grow fat and juicy.

They'd seen people and dogs and kids a' goin' up and down that beach right in front of em'. They'd studied sea shells and watched little crabs a' runnin' around. They'd listened to the boats a' partin' the water and the lonesome sound of the water slappin' up on the sand at night. They'd seen the lights of the ferries a' cuttin' through the dark.

Then it come to me. Them' berries was observers like the old prophets was, the ones that wore purple and never spoke and never come down from their mountains. Well, I come along and helped em' to take a little trip.

I already knowed what I was gonna' do with em'. I'd thought about it while I was cookin' em'. I was gonna' send every one of youn's' that crossed my mind a jar of blackberry beach jam.

The one's that's gone on is gittin' one in my

mind, and the rest of you I have always held dear is gonna' get a real one. That's how come you to git' this little package!

Well, I hope you all miss me as much as I miss you! My My! The time keeps flyin' by and summer's gone sa' quick, and we still ain't back together yet.

Well, you all take care of yourselves and do the best you can. Eat your blackberry jam with hot biscuits in the mornin' and I'll pretend I'm settin' right there with you.

2.   **Randy Purvis**

Dear Family,

Well, I take pen in hand to write to you again. I hope you're all a' farin' well and your summer was good.

Fall was allus' a restless time fer' us.... Remember us all a' pilin' into anything that would go, and settin' out? We didn't care where we went, jist' as long as we got gone.

Remember Abe Frank, that tall drink of water and how he always was a' talkin' and restless? Arnie's a lot like that. Arnie always knows where he is, but sometimes he don't know why he's there, and I have to remind him. That's 'cause of that stuff him and them men smoke. He does very well at plenty of things, but he completely misses the mark on others.

One day awhile back, Arnie was gone to work. I was listenin' to the radio and a' soakin' that rum cake Arnie likes sa' much when it come on the radio about the state fair. They announced that the Melody Brothers was gonna' be there.

I'm a' tellin' you, I got all shook up. As quick as Arnie got in the door from work, I told him I had to go see em'. The only big star I like better than them is that fine singin' man, that velvet eyed ramblin' crooner Randy Purvis!

Arnie said he'd try to get tickets for us, so I went to waitin'. I waited and waited. He never said a word so I knew he'd forgot all about it. He's bad to forget things from all that smokin' he does.

Now Arnie, he don't like the kind of music I do. He was raised in a big city with a bunch of places to go to and listen to music. He says his taste is more refined than mine. He can rattle off all the singers and the words to any song he likes, old or new, jist' like he does with all them sports facts. He sounds like one of them radio sports announcers when he gets started.

Arnie's favorite band in the whole world is called The Moody Dudes. He's seen em' a whole bunch of times, and he never gets tired of em'. He has all their music. He's played it fer' me, but there's too many of em' a' singin' at odd times and a' talkin', and I couldn't catch on to what them trips was that they was always a' takin'. Arnie says I don't understand the deeper meanings of life.

Anyway, that radio station announcer was talkin' about the state fair concerts, and who all was gonna' be there, but Arnie said he never heard them say anything about the Melody Brothers. He thought they said the Moody Dudes was gonna' be there, so he called in and ordered tickets.

By the time he got home from playing basketball and smokin' with his men friends, he told me he'd ordered Melody Brothers tickets. We was to pick them up at the state fair ticket counter when we went on Tuesday night. Then we could go right in and watch them.

He drove us the twenty miles and we stood in line on Tuesday night. When we got up to the ticket window, the lady inside told Arnie that he'd ordered tickets for the next night to see

Randy Purvis.

She said the Melody Brothers was sold out, and the Moody Dudes wasn't gonna' be there at all. I listened to her and jumped up and down and laughed about it. Arnie had done things like this before, but this was a good one.

I told Arnie that he was for sure gonna' bring me back the next night so's I could see that fine, velvet eyed, strong jawed, handsome Randy Purvis singin' in person.

I was ready to go home, but Arnie went to arguin' with the ticket lady. He likes to argue. He calls it debatin'. I could see he felt pretty bad about his mix-up.

I stood around awhile waitin' on the argument to end but Arnie wouldn't quit, so leaned over the ticket counter, jumped in the middle of the argument, and asked her who was gonna' be on the show tonight since we was already here.

She said yes, she still had tickets left. She said this little old band that used to be around a long time ago that nobody much remembered these days. I asked who it was, and she said Crepter Zen Maniac! I give her a look of pity. She was too young to know any better. Well, they was just us kids favorite rock and roll band in the whole world while we was a' growin' up, remember?

They sung songs about the Vietnam war and some kind of rain that scalded your skin, and how to be a good man when you grew up.

I thought all of them was pretty good men back then, and I still knowed every one of their songs by heart.

Arnie grumbled somethin' about them bein' a burger band instead of a steak band, whatever that means, but we got the tickets and went in to watch em' anyway.

We climbed right up in them bleachers and set down and waited. The sun went down. The stars come out and went to shinin' long about the time Crepter Zen Maniac run out on stage.

I never set down one time after they started singin'. I sung and danced in the aisle up in them bleachers under them stars with all of you I'd growed up with. I remembered doin' the hoedown and all the old dances that come to us so easy back then. I grinned at youn's in the dark and laughed.

Arnie got off his high horse when he seen I didn't give a damn about his opinion right then. Same way we felt back in young days about some of our warty kin. When he saw that everybody around us was a' carryin' on the same way I was, he got started. All of you'ns and that fool Arnie and me danced just like the teenagers we was way back when they first sung them songs.

The next night, we went back to see that stage strollin', smooth voiced Randy Purvis. We had good seats down front that Arnie'd paid fer' when he thought he a' was buying Moody Dude tickets.

I wore my best clothes and put on a little lipstick just in case Randy got a good look at me. That Randy Purvis sure looked fine and tan and white toothed up on that stage underneath them twinklin' stars, and he sung like a manly angel put here on Earth fer' some good woman, too bad it ain't me. Ha ha.

It was Arnie's first country music concert, and he had a pretty good time. When we got home, he went to straight to sleep, but I stayed up late, writin' a little poem about that fine, word drippin', song sippin' Randy Purvis before I went to bed. I made the poem to match Arnie's snorin'.

Now Randy, don't forget me,
I'm a' waitin' in line,
I gave you my number,
but you lost it last time,
The songs that you sing,
bring love to my heart,
Oh, Randy, a ring,
and we never shall part

Next month, we're gonna' see the Moody Dudes, so me and Arnie both git' ta' see ever' body we wanted to.

Well, I've run out of paper, so all youn's take care, and drop me a line when ye' can!

3.   Maisie

"Tonight I'm gonna' have turnip greens from the garden for supper. I'm gonna' fry up some fatback real crisp and bake a cake of cornbread to go with 'em. Ye' kin stay if ye' want.

While supper's coolin' off, I'm a' gonna' set on the porch and study them trees that's growed up over that little path I took as a kid to git' to the head of that holler up above here. Ye' cain't hardly find the way no more!

My goodness! My feet wore that path out when I was a young'in, and Mommy and Daddy wanted me to stay right here night and day and work around the old home place!

I remember old Marthy Glickson. She lived up in that holler. She made her home up there all by herself. Her cabin was built by that Chase Jackson bunch a long time ago. She moved into the abandoned cabin and took up livin' up there long before I was born. She never troubled nobody fer' nothin'.

She never troubled nobody when she died neither. She must a' had some a' them Indian people around, 'cause we found her all nice and tidy, laid out peaceful as can be and dry as a bone a' layin' up on one of them racks them Indians put their dead people up on.

We never said a word to nobody about findin' her. We just passed her burial place on by, Mommy and me, like it wasn't even there. But I remember Mommy a' pickin' a briar rose, purtiest wild flower you ever seen, all pink and green, and her a' tossin' it up on Marthy's burial rack before we went on.

Now, I got a little Indian in me, too, and I been a' thinkin' I wouldn't mind one little bit a' goin' like Marthy Glickson went. I'm kind a' likin' the thought of it.

Back when I was young, them Indians was around all the time when I played up in the head of that holler. I always knowed I wouldn't see em', even if I looked, so I jist' went on about my business a' makin' little stick people so's I'd have somebody to talk to and not be sa' lonesome.

Here lately I've heard them a' beatin' on them ol' drums agin' up there. And well, ye' know, I jist' kind of like that sound. It sets good with the way I been a' feelin' lately.

Ye' can still hear em' a' singin' ever now and agin' when the wind blows jist' right. But ye' have to listen real close.

Grandmaw used to lay claim to them now and agin', but Grandpaw and none of the rest of the bunch would talk about our Indian heritage. I guess the folks down below at church convinced ever body the Indians was all heathen's!

Well, there ain't nobody but me left here on the old home place, an' I figure I've done my job here purty' well. I done everything I could fer' the chilern' and that old man of mine, and now ever one of em's gone off someplace else and left me here ta' fend fer' myself. Yep. There's only me to do for and answer to.

It's got awful lonesome and quiet around here, and I been a' thinkin' about ever thing, and

you know, I've purty' well made up my mind. I'm'
a' gonna' go back up in that holler and try to
find them Indians.

Maybe there's some a' them still a' drummin'
up there that saw me when I was a young'un a'
playin' up there. Mayhap they'll remember how
peart' I was, and take me over and teach me ta'
saing' and daince' like I never could down at that
little church below here.

And I'm a' hopin' that when the time comes
fer' me ta' go, that they'll help me to look as
peaceful as old Marthy Glickson did a' layin' up
high in the air like she was, a smile dried up
right purty' on her face, and her a' holdin' a bag
of parched corn so she wouldn't git' hungry on
her way to the Promised Land.

Lordy, look at that sun! Hit's almost gone! I
guess I better git' back in the house and start
supper!

Thank ye' fer' stoppin' by. I kin' see it
wouldn't do any good ta' ast' ye' to stay. Ya' don't
need ta' tarry, fer' I see that yer' in a hurry ta'
get out of these old hills before dark falls. I don't
blame ye one bit. Go on, now. Go before it git's
too dark to leave here. Bye Bye."

4. Isolation

It's hard to be with anyone else when you're in a crowd all the time. Especially when Josie, curled up over there in the corner, says she just had a baby, and Teresa, we know she had nine. Corrine keeps borrowing my black Capri pants without asking me, and Stella keeps changing the sheets, and Susan keeps doing the laundry whether it's dirty or not.

Sometimes I think I am the only sane one of the bunch, at least until the nurse comes in with another pink pill.

Once I tried to talk them into taking a trip out of here, but Shelley started searching for her smelling salts and said she needed to store her suitcase at the greyhound bus station in a locker before we left town. Jenny wanted to hide her money under the mattress until we got back, and I told her I couldn't sleep on a lumpy bed, that I was like the princess in The Princess and the Pea story, and then I had to tell her the story, because she didn't know what I was talking about.

Joanie said she needed to color her hair first, because blondes have more fun, she was tired of it being white, and Nina wanted to go to the basement and bring up her matched set of lucky luggage—the ones she took to Acapulco a long time ago when she met that man, the one who carried them to her room and stayed all night- but I told her there was no basement in this place, just room after room after room full of old ladies.

None of them would listen, so after a while, I got tired of their planning instead of doing and gave up. I said we should go to a movie instead of trying to take a trip out of here. They finally shut up like they do every damn day we spend in this place, so I turned the television back on and tried to find Ginger and Fred before the "helpers" got here and turned off the black and white movies we all like to watch, and turned the television set back on that damned bad news channel they like to watch every day.

5.   A Modified Sinner

Lola Mertz lived in the north side of the shabby, one story duplex. Aunt Roxie, my mother's oldest sister, my favorite aunt, lived in the south side of their shared house.

I stood on the broken sidewalk in front of the dried out, postage stamp size front yard studying their house, worn suitcase in hand, listening to the bus that just dropped me off wind it's noisy way out of sight. I shuddered and mumbled under my breath in protest.

"Did all leavings have to be so damn noisy?"

The house Lola Mertz and Aunt Roxie lived in was one in a long row of rental shotgun duplexes that had seen better days when better days were already old. The newly built row of wood houses once looked fresh and exciting to the young and eager prospective tenants of the Fifties.

The neglect of many greedy landlords showed up along the row of houses; A long crack in the concrete, a chunk of sidewalk shoved up and displaced by a large tree root from one of the tall pecan trees growing behind the duplexes. A bottom corner of the house next door rested almost on the ground. Signs of wood being ambitiously termite ridden and ignored except by a large family of stray, multi-colored cats, were just the highlights.

Their house was painted a chalky mint green, the latest in a long line of cheap, colorful paint jobs slapped over flaking wood. Fresh paint meant to cheer up the tenants who apparently were frequently cheerless. Thin coats of amazing colors layered beneath the latest skimpy coat of paint shone through in an unusual rainbow effect when the sun moved across the sky on sunny days. The sunlight caused the house to look like a badly frosted icebox cake melting slowly on its pedestal during an outdoor southern church social on a hundred degree day.

Like older southern ladies, powdered, rouged, and sitting on the porch sipping their cold, tall, condensation fogged glasses of lemonade on a muggy Sunday afternoon, the row of shotgun duplexes wore their thin, proper veneers like Sunday go to meeting dresses with the utmost of proper, fragile dignity covering their old age. Almost sheer and see through, their many disabilities could be sensed lurking just under their surfaces.

Concrete "stoops," which Aunt Roxie and Lola Mertz, making the best of things, generously re-labeled "verandaahhs," were nestled in front of each front and back door, exuding heat in the summer, and nose freezing cold in the winter. High above each stoop floated a tiny v-shaped square of roof propped up with two long, thin posts. The posts were painted whatever color was left over from the latest house painting. The back of each tiny roof was toe-nailed to the house itself. It's faded patches of stoop shingles were erected once upon a time with the praiseworthy mission of offering shade.

Tall, gracious pecan trees grew in every backyard along the street. They provided the shade the little front porches couldn't. The trees were planted long ago by a landlord who hoped to see a profit from them after they matured.

The landlords that came and went were dissatisfied with that choice of future lucrative produce. Ever since the first nuts fell to the ground, riddled with holes from some kind of pecan predator that bore a fuzzy tail, the pecans were a disappointment. Besides, picking pecans, whether off the ground or from the tree, was back breaking work highly disapproved of by the plentiful squirrels who stayed fat and sassy from eating them.

To Aunt Roxie and Lola Mertz though, the sight of the tall, stalwart, back yard pecan trees conjured up memories of themselves in better days. Days of mint juleps, dainty sandwiches, and good-smelling beaux lolling half-drunk beneath shady old, nutty pecan tree branches.

Lola Mertz and Aunt Roxie's duplex stood third from the corner on what looked like a quiet, staid, residential street. Each duplex was overhung with deep shade in the generous back yards while deep sunlight parched the treeless, tiny front yards. It looked the picture of a place where age reigned in the deep silence of quaintness and tranquility. But it wasn't.

It has been observed by many that, "Looks can be deceptive." I have personal experience of that being true with most of the gentlemen I have sequestered myself with as I am making my way through life.

In front of the long row of duplex houses ran a two lane, blacktopped street that shot straight as an arrow, as though Robin Hood himself held the bow, into the city's central post office. Racing engines broke the tranquility all day long, for most of the postal customers used the street as a racetrack to speed straight into the postal parking lot, barring rain, sleet or snow; even when the road was iced and should have been more perilous than a day of no mail.

÷

Aunt Roxie and Lola Mertz met when they were young wives with small children. Back then, they never gave a thought to the future or what might become of them when they grew old. Time rolled gently past, full of stiff, sugar laced doilies with high ruffles, sitting importantly under cut-glass lamps; fragrant pot roast dinners prepared between scrubbing toilets, folding flat white sheets smelling of sunshine; sprinkling and ironing clothes; kids climbing trees, running in and out from their green, wide front yards to the backyard swings and climbing trees; and husbands who nodded off to sleep at night in front of tiny television screens in what were known as "dens."

Of course, Aunt Roxie, true southern maven, would not utter the "t" word. She would whisper "commode," if push came to plunger, never "t----t." Besides, "commode" was a 14-point Scrabble® word, while the other word was merely a 6-pointer.

Suddenly the families they raised were gone, and the husbands too. Over forty years gone by in the blink of an eye. Aunt Roxie aspired to the stage in her younger days, spending much of her time insouciantly dreaming of starring as a southern belle in a movie with Ronald Coleman or Errol Flynn. She would have been a natural at it, she informed anyone who asked, in her deep southern drawl. That dream vanished like the hot steams vanished from the still behind old man Hershel's place every morning the very instant she met H.W. Welch, automobile salesman.

Before a month was past, she was swept off her feet and carried away into connubial bliss with the new, dark haired, discreetly mustached, spats wearing, young salesman from Atlanta, now employed down at Henry Abelson's New and Genteelly Used Vehicle Haven.

She quickly became a wife to one magnificent man—her words—and a dedicated Mama to seven pretty little ladies; Willa Scarlett, Alice Caroline, Lucy Georgia, Delft Magnolia, Rose Delta, Vivian Lee, and Susannah May. Each one arrived slowly and sedately as was proper, home births, all in the middle of summer, precisely two years apart, except for Vivian Lee, who debuted by showing up six months earlier than two years, almost throwing the lineage out of place. When Aunt Roxie rose from her birthing bed, she had a firm talk with Mr. Welch about impulsive, unadvised amour in private under the magnolia trees out back of their commodious, two story home. That very day, everything went back to being the way it should be.

She raised her girls with an iron hand hidden beneath pink and purple silk ruffles—her two favorite colors—all worn while lifting skillets or ironing a blouse or cleaning something.

Mr. Welch was so flabbergasted and

overwhelmed by his good luck at home, that he stayed at work all the time and made lots of money. He quickly became a city council member, volunteer fire fighter, a habitual volunteer for anything away from home, while Aunt Roxie, afternoon dress perfect, gloved, hatted and shoed, with matching handbag, diligently searched for yet another one of her beloved land yachts in her spare time.

H.W. secretly ate at the local diner where they took pity on him and didn't tell on him. Aunt Roxie ignored Mr. Welch and kept on cooking, she and her seven girls, serving burnt and ill-advised foods to each other, causing their temperaments to suffer alarming lapses in good manners, which is where I came in.

When we were young, my seven cousins deigned to speak to me once in a while, usually about my deportment, lack of white gloves, and my predilection for becoming a slut when I grew up. Eventually, each of the Welch home grown debutantes grew up and found a besotted southern gentlemen to marry and moved away, one by one. I was most grateful as their unwanted, prurient interest in me abated.

Alas, after decades of contented marital bliss, though minus her girl's household and cooking skills, Aunt Roxie and her husband's life together ended abruptly one fine Saturday evening when H. W. had a heart attack at the dining room table while eating dinner. It was the final, fatal blow following an over-extended wrestling match with the large, succulent, but extremely tough pot roast Auntie had prepared.

One accepted their cooks for better or worse,

and even though Mr. Welch offered to pay for a spare cook many times, Aunt Roxie always spurned his generosity out of modesty. She was a stubborn woman, and she remained stubborn to and through his demise.

÷

Aunt Roxie and Lola Mertz shared more common threads and habits in their lives than tangled webs. All their children and both their husbands had flown the nest, so to speak. The children opted for moving long distances away after paying large dental bills and complaining about stomach problems, while the husbands followed H.W.s example and left on eternal quests for their own versions of a better land.

Though the two of them were as far apart as May of one year and December of the next in temperament about the philosophical accoutrements of life, their differences never stopped their friendship from flowering.

They sold their homes and went on countless senior cruise ships to every place they could think of, during which Lola Mertz took up the habit of using long, ornate cigarette holders. With a little practice, she no longer burned the eyebrows of anyone who hovered a bit too near when she smoked.

After they stopped wining and dining the old men on the senior cruise ships and playing bingo and gambling in every casino in the south, they ran out of money, so they finished out their sea-faring days playing Scrabble®.

On dry land again, sober and broke, the two

well-traveled but world-weary women, used their pensions to rent each side of the duplex located just a short distance from the busy main post office entrance.

÷

Living side by side was idyllic, but there was a bumpy, unfortunate beginning during which they were forced to cohabitate in one side of the duplex together for a short time. The old saying, "opposites attract," kicked in like it was stranded on the hard concrete front stoop way too long. The situation ended with their unspoken agreement to neva', neva' hate nor bludgeon one another. They would endure.

Then Auntie moved her bureau and other accoutrements into her own place next door. It happened just in the nick of time, too. Sometimes, opposites bring balance and relief only from a comfortable distance, or it seemed to be so with Auntie and Lola Mertz.

÷

All the duplexes on the street were identical. Inside each one was a short, wide front room with a wide border of wallpaper pasted to the back wall. The wallpaper border was the same in each duplex. It bore numerous bunches of large, lurid, overripe purple grapes ensconced in leaves and vines, encouraging an instant, strong, unspoken urge to imbibe as soon as one stepped into the living room. The thin walls of the duplexes were painted a stale off-white. The floors were worn wood, except for the kitchens, which boasted white linoleum thick and yellow from the many hopeful wax jobs guaranteed to, "Keep that shine for a lifetime!"

There was just enough room to turn around in the kitchen. The sparse counter space was parceled out around the white stove, ancient refrigerator, and chipped white sink.

Behind the right side of the living room lurked a tiny, closet sized bathroom with a tiny tub and no shower. Behind the left side was a small afterthought of a dining room leading into the kitchen at the rear of the duplex. The ladies kept their washers, dryers, and ironing boards in their dining rooms, more or less.

The one bedroom located at the back of the house behind the bathroom, boasted a thin, skinny window overlooking the panorama of a dismal, weed choked backyard. A rickety metal fence resembling worn out chicken wire swayed back and forth behind the tall weeds, looking like it was trying to make up its mind whether to fall forward or backward, yet never doing either, causing a high degree of suspense in the howling neighborhood dogs when the wind blew. The fence wound its unlovely, wavering, complaining way around the backyards, marking off here and there where the yard ended and the alley, filled with metal trash cans and Mr. Patterson's leftover car parts, began.

Aunt Roxie was the opposite of Lola Mertz. Aunt Roxie claimed she was now a rolling stone. Yes, she may have once been a simpering Southern Belle with a coming-out ball and a lily-white, freckle-less complexion, but she was bit decades earlier by the need to "express mah-self more fully." Forced to live with Lola Mertz for two months while the other side of the duplex was being renovated, she said it was all she could do to keep her sanity and not murder Miss Lola Mertz, "The Hoarder."

"I will always travel light," Aunt Roxie said. It was her Philosophy of Life A.D., meaning after she lost her roots, meaning after Mr. H.W. Welch's downward demise into the pot roast on a tranquil but gusty Saturday evening.

She retained just enough "accoutrements" in her half of the duplex to keep going. She owned twin beds, (hopeful, that was), a small table, a handful of dishes, a microwave oven, her clothes and other cosmetic supplies. Her duplex was neat and clean and quick, just as she had become. Aunt Roxie was short, small boned, hefty, and very stubborn. I was careful to never cross her unless it was absolutely necessary.

"At least I'm taller than Napoleon and a hell of a lot better looking, too!" she exclaimed, stating that was a quote from an obscure black and white movie. Her short, curly hair stood out from her head in a panorama resembling an angry sunset. The colors changed, depending on what hair color was on sale down at the Beauty Supply Warehouse, and how many boxes of it there were.

To her credit or discredit, Lola Mertz had "Intention" with a capital "I". She was proud of it, and mightily pleased that it was self-mesmerizing, not noticing that it gave her an air of acute senility in the eyes of many observers. She believed herself to be more intelligent than most, a factoid borne out because her half of the house was crammed with thousands of romance novels, cheap, obscure travel books, odd furniture clumped together, movie magazines, and food wrappers.

Lola Mertz walked slowly and ponderously through life, allowing time for her many layers of weightiness to seek their own levels. She talked slowly, deliberately, with long silences between her words, for she intended to stay emphatic. She spoke continuously and nonstop in a low monotone to anyone who appeared to listen, including the neighborhood dogs whom she cornered when she couldn't find anyone else when the wind wasn't blowing. She planned everything that didn't matter, ignored the things that did, and constantly entertained dense, negative thoughts, impressing herself, throwing her into various states of euphoric inertia, while depressing everyone else within earshot.

A recent and particularly toxic train of thought circled the question: "What if I was evah' in a serious, nearly fatal vehicular accident and had not donned clean and ironed underwear before the event?" That poser sparked a shudder of disgust among the two church ladies living in the duplex next door, specifically Miss Minnie Owens and Miss Bessie Phillips, loud and devout prayer makers.

÷

Miss Minnie and Miss Bessie prayed loudly with their windows open a minimum of twice a day for Aunt Roxie and Lola Mertz. Their loud

29

prayers informed the two world travelers at least twice a day that they would have nothing to do with the two miscreants unless they changed their slatternly, lustful, wanton ways and became civil, decent, God-fearing, chaste women, justly and sedately waiting for heaven to claim them, just as heaven had claimed their husbands who were waiting for them. But no—those two were just plain hussies who didn't want to be good. They were just looking for old men and playing Scrabble, one of the devil's games.

"They eschew us," Lola said to Aunt Roxie one day.

"Yes, dear, they do, and 'eschew' is worth 14 points on our Scrabble board, so get over it." Aunt Roxie replied, resolutely adding an "E" and a "D" to Lola's 'eschew' in a surreptitious coup.

The two devout ladies watched Aunt Roxie and Lola Mertz with ecumenical zeal from behind their white lace curtains, beginning with their arrival on Lola's front stoop each morning until they retired for the night.

I noticed their white lace curtains moving, and realized they were watching me. I started up the sidewalk, my worn, boxy brown suitcase bumping against my side. Aunt Roxie came out to meet me.

"What y'all standing out here for? Gatherin' moss?" she asked in a southern drawl thicker than molasses. "Come in the house and we'll get you settled in and have a good, long visit."

She took my arm and strolled us up the short sidewalk like she was headed toward the double doors of a fine plantation mansion while she glared at the moving white lace curtains in the open window next door on the left.

I heard the voices of Miss Minnie and Miss Bessie rise in protest and prayer between Aunt Roxie's words to me and, "oh, my sweet Baby Lord Jesus, they've called that fallen woman back in to join their demonic ranks!"

Aunt Roxie interrupted their rising voices. "Did I evah' tell you how I came to live in this house?" she asked loudly as we strolled up the porch steps. I'd heard the story before, but wisely decided to not mention times past just at that moment. I shook my head no.

Inside, she walked us into the bedroom, pulled my suitcase from my hand and planted it firmly on the other twin bed before she hugged me and clucked at me sympathetically.

'So, your show has left town again?"

"Six months ago," I choked out.

My "show" was what Aunt Roxie always called my latest boyfriend. She studied me a minute with world weary, shrewd eyes, then picked up where she left off with her story.

In a rich, syrupy voice, she said, "Ah' moved in with Lola Mertz so we could each survive a little bettah'. Ah' was livin' in Motha''s tiny old house with those damn curvy floors and that ancient sink, and the sweet, sharp smell of permanent dry rot." She shuddered. "Ah' couldn't take it anymore."

At that moment, Aunt Roxie got that familiar, far-away look in her eyes, the one that told me she was "missin' the lovely smellin' magnolias Daddy raised out back with such pride and allergic apoplexy."

She cut back her words and sighed deeply. The family wash swung silently in the summer air between us, some of it hanging still and some of it moving pretty fast in the breeze coming through the skinny bedroom window. Neither one of us said a word about anything. Neither one of us wanted to pull nary a clothes pin off of that eternal clothesline.

After a long silence, she said, "Ah' took the back bedroom ovah' there." She waved a hand at Lola Mertz's wall and continued, "Lola Mertz sleeps on a double bed in a corner of the living room. She leaves every light in the house on all night, and the television blasting. Well, this old place has bad plumbing and NO insulation forever! There were big gaps around her windows that the air blew through! Her utility bills were sky high because she was too lazy to plastic them over to keep the air in, or out, as the case might be."

Aunt Roxie nodded vigorously, a stubborn set to her jaw.

A picture came unbidden to me of Lola Mertz tucked up in her living room bed, stabbing a cigarette into a holder. She lay, heavy boned, weighty and officious, propped up on pillows, her long, straight, gray hair coiled around her head and shoulders like a dead or comatose cat. Her small, faded blue eyes darted about, while her pudgy nose sniffed the air, her thin, troubled mouth holding back a dam of words.

She waved her cigarette holder around in her pudgy hands so everyone would notice she wore matching lipstick and long red fingernails. Lola Mertz believed her cigarette holder made her look "elegant," like most of her southern childhood role models. This caused no end of both troubling shame and ensuing defiance for her, for everybody knew southern ladies should nevah, nevah, nevah smoke, nevah' laugh at racy jokes, nevah' wear black in summer, nevah' imbibe gin on hot afternoons, and nevah' go anywhere without a freshly ironed lace hankie in their purse!

"Ah' told her that Ah' wasn't going to pay a dime of the utility bills because of it. But you know how Lola Mertz is. Her nature is morose at best, and she just said, "Whatever."

I nodded my head solemnly but didn't answer. Lola Mertz was not someone I was close to, even though she was my Aunt Roxie's best friend, and we'd been acquainted most of my life. Lola Mertz was heavy boned, with specific layers of fat she pampered and petted, daubing Oils of Things over the round white handles above her hips.

She slept when she wasn't reading a romance novel, movie magazines, or rummaging around in a food container. She could talk for hours about a salt shaker, or whether "founder" was a verb.

Aunt Roxie interrupted my thoughts.

"Ah' told her, you couldn't fall down fast! You'll be late for your own funeral!"

By then, my suitcase was empty, my things in place on the dresser top and in the proper drawers.

"Let's go set a spell on the "verandaahh," Aunt Roxie said, waving an arm in the direction of the stoop out front, meaning the four by five feet concrete porch with three concrete steps leading down to the skinny concrete sidewalk.

She took my arm and we sashayed outside just as Lola Mertz stepped ponderously out on her porch. Aunt Roxie stopped talking while Lola Mertz solemnly picked out a place to sit, then motioned for us to come over and join her. The small patch of shade over Lola Mertz's front porch was most welcome.

Aunt Roxie and Lola Mertz both wore colorful, large floral mumus for comfort in the heat, their hair up in rollers, fluffy bright colored mules on their swollen feet. They eyed my cuffed up jeans and white blouse with disfavor, but never said a word.

"Sometimes actions speak louder than words!" I piped up pertly.

The two of them eyeballed each other.

"We sure hope so!" Auntie answered snappily.

I knew when to shut up and did. They would always believe pants were for boys, while I would always beg to differ.

Sighing gustily, they propped their feet up on a couple of old paint cans they'd found in the dilapidated shed out back of the house. Once they were settled in, they exhaled like old divas, and fanned their sweaty faces.

I knew their routine. Each day they sat on the tiny porch, watching the drivers whiz by on their way to and from the post office. They kept busy by snapping green beans for dinner, reading romance novels to each other while chain smoking, or applying more red lipstick, and playing their never ending game of Scrabble.

They watched the superior, aggressive

mothers whizzing by in their SUVs, their whiny children strapped into car seats, demanding more, more, more, as their crazed mothers swung into the post office to drop important letters into the blue metal boxes while chattering on their cell phones in their high, strident voices.

"They sound like nails scrapin' on a chalkboard," Lola Mertz complained, noting that "chalkboard" was a 22-point Scrabble word, without any folderol of double-letter tiles or double word bonuses.

They watched the immigrant kids, fresh and hopeful in the mornings as they walked down the street to the Catholic school, then in the afternoon, tired and relieved as they trudged home past the porch.

They watched them all, the poor kids wearing Salvation Army jeans, the busy, self-important young wives, the hurrying, middle aged professionals pushing forward, the stray dogs and wandering cats, and the shooed away tired salesmen.

They watched the rich, complex life flowing past the duplex in between bluing their white clothes and voicing strong opinions about meatloaf. When I was visiting, I always watched with them.

But life was changed since the last time I visited. Now there were new favorites to keep an eye on. New favorites they yearned to interact with, favorites who did not disturb or froth up their sympathy or pity.

Aunt Roxie smiled at me. Ladies didn't grin; they smiled. Grinning was for Cheshire cats.

"Should ah' tell her, Lola?"

Lola Mertz pondered the question a long while, then nodded slowly.

Aunt Roxie said with vast amusement in a syrupy southern drawl, "Well, dear girl, we have taken up watching a new, refined clientele that we have much more in common with. The old men who drive by from the new retirement "home" the "gova-mint" built recently three blocks from heah', ovah' on Chancell Street! How about that?"

I sat in silence, not knowing what answer she wanted. I just nodded and squinted up at her from my concrete seat on the top "verandaahh" step.

The silence went on for another minute before Aunt Roxie broke it to ask, "Ah'm wonderin' where we can find a couple of those lawn chairs, you know, the kind with the canopy on top and a cup holda' on the side?"

Lola Mertz snorted in response. Aunt Roxie smiled at me. We both knew Lola Mertz got mad if another person got an especially bright idea before she did.

Finally I asked, "What for?"

"So we can investigate our new circumstances further in a more comfortable style." Aunt Roxie answered, looking at me like I was dull witted.

"What circumstances?" I asked. She looked at me with pity.

"The men!" she exclaimed and sighed gustily.

"Let me explain the situation to you. At first, we didn't know where all those old men came from, and we didn't care!" She pressed her hand to her ample bosom. "Ah' myself was just thankful to Jesus, or whoeva' one calls whateva', and just happy to throw my eyes on 'em! Manna from Heaven!"

I smiled at her with both longing and understanding. All three of us sighed at the same time. A lengthy silence filled with sadness for our losses and hopes for our futures dragged on until Auntie spoke again.

"Anywhooo..., me and Lola Mertz got to talkin' about how we might like to have companions again, now that we're fully retired and have extra time on our hands."

I nodded again.

Aunt Roxie continued, "You know, we have earned the special natures we now have. We're more mature these days. We are wiser, full of strategically located wrinkles, and bereft of unreasonable sin. Life ain't long enough to gather enough sins to please a body! And ah' don't like bein' just a modified sinner! Ah' want to be a flame bustin', all out, plain old, four square sinner! Ah' told Lola Mertz it requires a good, strong man to partake in all of that and keep up with it! Ah' want to look forward to dancin' in Hell's flames with a hell of a lot of good memories keepin' me company! Lola Mertz don't like me talkin' like that, but it's the damn truth!"

I laughed while Aunt Roxie smiled expansively at me. She was a natural born storyteller and dearly loved a good audience. She expanded further.

"We are advantageously located here!" she announced, waving an arm up at the overhanging branches of the pecan trees, then out at the sun soaked, tiny front yard.

"The old men's home is really an upscale, new retirement complex for refined older gentlemen," she announced, as though she was reading from a slick, tri-fold brochure. "Full of mature men."

Lola Mertz snorted. Aunt Roxie ignored her and went on, "Upscale because most of them have a car and can still drive, and they have to drive down our street right past us to get to the post office!"

"Or through the alley," Lola Mertz noted dryly.

Aunt Roxie glared at her and huffed. "Well! They would all have flat tires and skinned paint jobs if they tried to get through there!"

She shook her head and smiled at me.

"They have to pass us out front, but one way or another, front or out back, we have become a force to be reckoned with!"

Lola Mertz didn't reply. She acted as though she didn't hear a word even though her thin lips quivered. I cocked my head to the side and studied her. Maybe she'd grown hard of hearing since the last time I visited. Did hearing tests and hearing aids loom on the horizon? Damn aging! One of the few moments I felt pity for her.

Aunt Roxie paused for effect.

"Which leaves us having the rare opportunity of picking and choosing the ones we like the best! We observe them from this location and they observe us. Nothing wrong with that, is there?"

She fixed me with a stare, waiting for my

confirmation. I felt like a specimen on a pin being stared at by Auntie-the-scientist through a high powered microscope before she decided how to display me in a talcum powder box lined with a dainty lace handkerchief. I nodded vigorously. I smiled, not grinning. She pulled her eyes away from me piece by piece after she was satisfied that my attitude had been corrected and restored.

She glared out at the street, staring at the hideous new speed bump repining in coal black and yellow striped glory across the blacktopped, two lane highway in front of their duplex.

"We call that thing the hallelujah speed bump now, but we didn't on the start. Before the city laid that speed bump down, everybody drove down our street like hell was chasin' em', like they were Charlton Heston in that Ben Hur horse race movie! Well, that speed bump sure slowed the old men from the retirement center down! Hallelujah!

"What about the rest?" I asked.

Auntie glared at me and said, "To heck with them! Me and Lola Mertz know when a good thing is right under our noses. Like a winning hand in a card game. Lola Mertz got busy and made up a list of things to say to the old men we favored, and we hollered them right out from this verandaahh'. We started out politely with, "How do you do?", "How are you today?" and 'How do you like the weather?"

I watched Aunt Roxie wind herself up like the boiler Humphrey Bogart kicked so it expelled its overload of steam in that movie with Katherine Hepburn.

"At first, the gentlemen from the retirement home gave us surprised looks until they realized we were going to be sitting out on this porch every day. At least when the weather is good.

We asked real nice questions, polite and all, but they ignored us, so we made the questions snappier. We started asking them things like, "Hot enough for you today?" "Made any plans for later?" or "Do you like fried chicken?"

Aunt Roxie looked over at Lola Mertz and narrowed her eyes a bit, "That one was her idea!"

I ignored the sudden vision of burnt fried chicken served from her table when I was young. Aunt Roxie shook her head mournfully and heaved a great sigh.

"But they kept on ignoring us and driving by faster and faster. So we got to thinking that maybe they couldn't hear us, so we got rid of the words. We shook our heads, crossed our arms or frowned or give them sappy looks and swooning stares. Like mimes, you know?"

She looked at me questioningly. I nodded and prayed not to grin.

"We blew big kisses at them, depending on our mood—whether we liked them that day or not. But it didn't impress the old gentlemen any more than our polite conversation which left out all the swear words on account of politeness and good manners!

Most of them sped up so much they deserved a ticket! They risked knocking off their mufflers when they plowed across that damned hallelujah speed bump. Some even tossed the finger at us, if you can believe that!"

I nodded my head again too vigorously, and

Auntie slanted another long, sideways look at me until I quit nodding. When that confrontation ended and I was put back in my place, Auntie sighed, reached in and adjusted a voluminous bra strap before she went on. She leaned back in her chair, heaved another sigh and waved a long, red-nailed finger around for effect. She waxed poetic.

"But things weren't so bad. The sweet summer dusk each day moved slowly into night, and in between, the sun shed light on the mature, silver tongued savages that whizzed by us on their way to the post office while we sat out here and looked them over with a view towards reviving one or two of them."

She would have continued waxing poetic but stopped to draw her breath after her long soliloquy.

Lola Mertz snorted and raised a dainty embroidered hanky to her thin, trembling lips and tapped them. I cocked my head sideways and studied her again. Her lips were trembling again? Wasn't that too soon for normal? Was she experiencing some kind of seizure?

I sighed and looked away. I needed to give up being so damn scared of this aging stuff. But, hell! It was going on all around me! People I knew, people I grew up with, people I once shacked up with, were dying off like flies! Well, none of the shack up jobs were my fault. None of them ever lasted long enough for me to give them a heart attack or apoplexy. I warned Rex about that ditzy blond before he left me! I heaved my own morose sigh.

Auntie studied me thoughtfully. We sat in

silence. I didn't want her to know too much, so I asked a question.

"When did they put that speed bump in?"

Aunt Roxie rolled her eyes over at Lola Mertz.

"They put it in the weekend Lola Mertz and ah' went on a trip. We came back and every damn thing was changed! We only drove fifty miles from here, but you'd have thought it was the end of the world when we got back!

We rode in that old land yacht of hers to visit her Aunt Prudence, who's kept one foot on a banana peel and the other in the grave for the last fifteen years. We stayed over through Monday, then drove back on Tuesday, carryin' that damn little bea-u-r-o that Lola Mertz's aunt bestowed upon her, in the trunk."

She shook her head back and forth in disapproval.

"It took Lola Mertz all day Monday to get that little thing wedged just the way she wanted it into the trunk of her land yacht. She wouldn't let me help one bit."

Aunt Roxie shook her head again. "She's stubborn as a mule! And it always costs us time! She's gonna' be late for her own funeral! She cain't fall down fast!"

Auntie was building up steam again.

Lola Mertz just sat there, waving a cardboard fan with a picture of Jesus on it slowly back and forth in front of her face, staring out at the hallelujah speed bump with a solemn gaze. Aunt Roxie's fan had Clark Gable's picture on it. I special ordered it for her last Christmas.

Suddenly, Lola Mertz sneezed loud enough to wake the dead. Auntie and I shouted, "Bless you!" in reactionary self-defense. Lola Mertz's thin lips calmed and stopped trembling as I watched. So that was it! Not a seizure. I laughed inwardly at myself. *"See what happens with your over active imagination?"*

I turned back to listen to Auntie.

"Anywhooo...we turned onto our street, and right in front of us loomed the biggest, ugliest, most God awful speed bump ah' have ever seen in my life!"

She shouted and pointed at the rounded asphalt line repining in yellow bumblebee-striped glory across the two lane street.

"We didn't know what the hell to do! Howdy Jones, were we ever mad!" Auntie and Lola Mertz both shook their fists at the uncaring bulge of lofty asphalt spread across the street like part of a huge, lazy snake.

"When Ah' saw that speed bump, God forgive me, Ah' took the Lord's name in vain! Ah' shouted "Jesus Christ! Mary, Joseph, and Jesus!"

Auntie looked at Lola Mertz.

"Well, Lola Mertz was forced to navigate her land yacht up and over that speed bump before she could turn into the driveway. It was like crossing a mountain. We both cussed all the way across it. We parked and got out of the car and looked at that thing, and I said that is NOT a regular speed bump! That is a G.D. speed bump pumped up on steroids!"

She caught her breath and glanced at me guiltily.

"You know what G.D. means, right?"

I nodded and responded pertly, "Gusty

Dinger!" A ready answer saved over from childhood days.

They rolled their eyes at each other, exchanging a quick, meaningful glance of pity before they looked at the speed bump again and shook their fists. Then Aunt Roxie leaned back, caught her breath, stuck out her little pinkie, and sipped daintily from her tall glass of lemonade. Aunt Roxie and Lola Mertz agreed heartily that "speed bump" was not only *not* a Scrabble® word, but it had no true synonym. Of course, 'synonym' was a gift-from-heaven Scrabble® word worth 15 points but you had to snag two of the four "y" tiles.

"Ah' know it's not ladylike to get so mad, but ah' was in such a state that Lola Mertz gave me two of her purple pills. We figure the Federal "gova mint" placed that speed bump there to slow people down because the post office is a "gova mint" facility, right? We did our best to put a curse on whoever put it there, hoping it would be gone by morning, but it didn't work.

At first, that speed bump held us hostage. We were forced to deal with it every G.D..." she caught her breath and glanced at me, "...Gusty Dinger... time we pulled in or out of the driveway. So we put off going to the Goodwill and the grocery store and church, and we both started eating too much and gaining weight and getting depressed. And it was all the fault of that no good, ugly giant mass of asphalt slap in front of our house!

Well, it took a little while, but we got tired of hating it and resigned ourselves to it being there longer than we would probably live."

Aunt Roxie laughed bitterly and breathlessly, clinking her lemonade glass against mine in an unexpected move. I watched a cool trickle of sweat trail slowly down the side of her glass.

"It won. We were blind to the blessings hidden in it on the start. But one day we both had a full blown epiphany, settin' right here. We realized God had heard finally our prayers after all of these years and decided to get off his duff and answer them at the last minute. Like all men, both God and the Federal govamint' works in mysterious ways."

"It took forty years' worth of prayers," Lola Mertz stated dryly. "Twenty years from each of us." They nodded wisely at each other.

÷

Lola Mertz took over. "Better late than never. Now Jesus doesn't have quite as much to answer for, because that speed bump forces every driver going down this street to slow down. Nobody can race down this street into the post office anymore, so the old men have to slow down, too! Get it?"

They both looked at me, then cackled triumphantly at the look on my face.

"So we have the opportunity to get a good look at every one of them!" they hooted.

"It is a glorious, monstrous, huge and ugly like a bad frog prince, a hallelujah of a speed bump! God placed that damn thing right in the perfect spot for us!"

Lola Mertz emphasized, waving her cigarette holder in circles, pointed it at the speed bump, then went silent. Aunt Roxie took over again.

"At first, we set on the porch here doing character studies of each of the older gentlemen passing by, but we were forced to keep moving our lawn chairs down the sidewalk to get a better look at them," Aunt Roxie said.

"We moved further and further down the sidewalk until we found the perfect spot."

She narrowed her eyes at the street as if measuring it. "It's six feet from the sidewalk to the edge of the speed bump, so that puts us about eight feet from each car."

She lifted her arms in the air like she was in a revival tent meeting, rolled her eyes heavenward, and shouted, "Thank you Jesus, for sending all those old men to us!"

Aunt Roxie dropped her head as if in prayer. Gratitude filled her face. Two tiny tears rolled down her cheeks.

I made a scoffing noise and thought to myself, "*Why, she hasn't prayed since before Jesus was born!*"

I fixed Auntie with a hard glare. She was a devout sinner, although a modified sinner these days, due to age and condition. She ignored my piercing stare. Eyes fastened on the huge, ugly, yellow-striped speed bump, she said, "My plan is to purchase Lola Mertz and me two new lawn chairs from DayMart so we can be more comfortable out there."

She made it sound like they were getting in supplies before going out in a jungle to hunt lions.

"Ah' want the kind of chairs that have the beverage holders and overhead shade covers.

And ah' plan to accessorize the shade part of the chairs with that ball of fringe left over from Mardi Gras back in the sixties in my sewing box. It's vintage. Then we can set the chairs closer to the curb so we can see the old men even better without getting sun burned or heat stroked.

Old men aren't likely to be attracted to a future of entrainment, so we must be careful to make it look like nothing permanent. It will look like we are just sunning ourselves, sipping lemonade and chatting.

It gets pretty hot out here, especially when some of them smile back at us. We'll need two extra chairs just in case a couple of them decide to stop awhile, and set with us. The men's chairs have to look inviting, kind of like a recliner."

A long silence stretched out while we sat in the dappled sunlight underneath the tiny porch roof. The post office was closed today, so no cars or school children were passing by.

Aunt Roxie glared down the street at the small, dilapidated, whitewashed wood edifice tilted at a crazy angle in the middle of the weed filled, empty lot beside the post office. She frowned at the hand painted sign nailed to the front it announcing in misspelled script, "Claire's Restrunt."

She sighed and shook her head in disapproval.

"For a while, Lola Mertz cooked. We carried lasagna out here and showed it to the men we favored when they drove by. We fanned the smell of it at their cars with our hands while they crossed the speed bump. But all that happened was Claire opened up that feeble excuse for a diner right beside the post office. And she's a mighty poor cook, so the old men pass back by here with sour looks on their faces after they eat there. It isn't our fault they got acid indigestion. All they needed to do was stop here, but you know how old men are. They can't cook for themselves, but still, they are deceptively hard to catch."

She shook her head and added wistfully, "Sometimes Ah' just want to cook for someone else again."

Lola Mertz and I groaned loudly and spontaneously.

Quickly Lola Mertz piped up, "'Indigestion' is worth 14 points you know, whereas 'reflux,' though shorter, is worth 18 points, dear."

Aunt Roxie rolled her eyes. A righteous tone crept into her voice. "But I quit cooking years ago, and now we've gone to playing Scrabble!"

Lola Mertz interrupted, announcing, "I'm going to the bathroom," which is worth 15 points, as you know, compared to 'restroom,' which is worth 10."

She struggled to her feet. Aunt Roxie watched until the door closed behind her. Then she turned to me and confided in a loud whisper, "She can't hear it thunder but ah'm patient with her 'cause she's turned out to be a hell of a lip reader! People talk to themselves while they're crossing that speed bump, and Lola Mertz reads their lips and tells me what they're saying!"

Auntie pursed her heavily lip-sticked mouth thoughtfully.

"Ah' think some of the people going down this street need a cake of soap took to their mouths, and a good church to pray in."

She shrugged at me and smiled. "Oh well, we can't help where we live, can we? We just have to deal with what we've been given..."

She rolled her eyes up towards heaven while I looked at her and nodded vigorously. She stopped and looked down at me suspiciously.

"What are you thinking?" she asked. "What you got on your mind?"

I said, " 'Mind' is a short word worth 6 points, but 'thinking' is worth 16 points because of the K, which is worth 5 points all by itself."

As if she read my mind, Aunt Roxie went on to say that "veraandaahh" was worth 15 points, just edging out "porch," which was worth a surprising 12 points, despite having fewer letters.

I rolled my eyes innocently at dear old Aunt Roxie. Years ago, we were ages apart, but now our worlds were much closer, especially since I hadn't been backstage at a "show" for a long time. Frankly, I was afraid that long time would turn into never again.

I looked at her and then out at that huge speed bump in the street and shuddered. It was the ugliest thing I ever saw, all yellow and black, but I kept my eyes pinned right on it.

I said, "Maybe I'll just pick up a lawn chair for myself when we go to DayMart."

"Hhhmmm..." Aunt Roxie studied me judiciously through her large, black rimmed rhinestone studded glasses, one finger tapping her pursed red lips, while I waited for her answer.

"Why don't we get you one of those cute little

flowered, hot pink overnight cases too? Lola Mertz and ah' each have one. We keep em' packed and ready to go. Then you can set it beside of your lawn chair just like we do."

I stared at her, puzzled. "What do you mean? Are you planning on taking a trip?"

Aunt Roxie waved her hand and laughed.

"Good Lord no! Even though I'm a rolling stone now. Not by ourselves again. It's just in case a couple of the men stop and want to take us on a trip. You never know with men."

I studied her face a minute while she stared back at me. Finally I realized she meant every word. I looked away. This wasn't the first time I'd visited Aunt Roxie; no, not at all. I returned every time my latest show left town. Somehow, it had turned into a habit. But they say three's a charm, and there were three of us forever and insistently hopeful ladies gracing Lola Mertz's front stoop right this minute, so I might get lucky again. Who knows? From where I sat, it looked like it was time to get a new show on the road.

After a while I said, "Do they carry those overnight cases in blue?" Then helpfully I added, "You know, they make a wall-sized Scrabble® board. What if we got one and set it up by the speed bump? You know, on a big, sturdy easel? It's like a puzzle, and not many folks can resist the lure of a good round of Scrabble®"

Lola Mertz, who'd returned from inside and Aunt Roxie smiled like smug southern tabby cats and gave a unified trill. "Time for a trip to DayMart!"

6. Thanksgiving Dinner at the Car Parts Factory

I remember that old Maudie Clutch very well.
I worked with her in that car parts factory up
north years ago. A lot of us southern women
worked in the car factories back then. Workin' in
them gives a woman grit. If you ain't got it when
you start, you'll git' it real quick.

Old Maude worked rings around the rest of
us. She was smart and old and short and
shaped like a basketball. She could count on
one hand the years left to go before her
retirement. Old Maude said whatever was on her
mind, any time she thought it, and sometimes it
cut pretty sharp. Her son was named Cliff, and
he was just as independent minded as she was.

We used to have a Thanksgiving dinner ever
year, us five women working up on the third
floor and each year we took turns bringing the
turkey.

I was never much of a cook, so the only kind
of roast turkey I knew about was the kind my
mother made. She put a giant turkey in the oven
with a clean white rag tented over the top of it,
and she basted it ever little while with butter
until it was brown all over and done. It took her
half the night and part of the next day to get it
done. It smelled real good, what you could smell
past all the smoke fillin' the kitchen while it was
a' bakin'. Now she didn't have no backbone left
from the way the old man done her, but she'd
fight him like a broody hen to have that turkey

51

ever year.

One year it was Old Maude's turn to cook the turkey for our Thanksgiving dinner. Maude did things her own way. She said she'd bought a tom turkey 'cause it was cheap. We'd never heard of cooking a tom turkey, only hen turkeys. She said toms were bigger than hens, with bigger bones. Then she barked out a short laugh. "Jist' like men!" she announced, rollin' her shrewd, faded blue eyes up to Heaven, leavin' out all kinds of things she might have said. That was Maude's way.

Maude wasn't a bit scared by that turkey being a tom. She didn't like to stay up all night for somethin' like roastin' a turkey, so she took her old blue enamel canner and slammed that old tom turkey in it and boiled it down on top of the stove. She put it on early in the mornin' the day of our dinner, and it was done in no time. We didn't know what to think when we saw Maude a' carryin' that blue speckled canner of turkey in. She slapped that canner dead center on our dinner table and grabbed the lid off. The steam rose off it. That old tom turkey was boiled to pieces. I sniffed the steam. I'll never forget the smell of salt and pepper and savory turkey. It wasn't a pretty sight, but it was the best turkey I ever smelled or tasted.

Janel brought Parker House rolls. They were fancy and shaped like rose tops. Janel was inclined to do things like that. Being around Janel and her classy ways made the rest of us women better than we had a right to be, though she was from the south, same as most everybody working in that car parts factory back then. Janel was tall, slim, and graceful, with olive skin, shiny brown hair, and sad brown eyes. She was kind, with good manners. She never told jokes or gossiped, but somehow, she kept us all a' smilin'. She was one of them women who never raised her voice like the rest of us did from time to time. She lived with her man in a big red brick house out in the country. Her man was a big, handsome feller from the south. They made a pretty pair. They had one girl named Jane, and Janel shopped at the best department stores up in the big city for herself and Jane's clothes. Red Bill, the guy who brought us the car parts we assembled, said her man run around on her, but I never believed him. She was too beautiful and too wise for anything like that to go on. I knew I could never be a lady like Janel. I'd already scrapped and fought too many low down battles in my short life. They'd made me too coarse, but Janel, she was refined in the best way I'd ever seen.

Phyliss and Wanda were sisters workin' up on the third floor with Janel, Margie, me and Old Maude. Wanda liked to quilt and clean and cook. She fit right in with the women of that time.

But Phyliss was a maverick. We admired her because she did what she wanted to. She liked to shop for clothes and go to social gatherings. She was the older of the two sisters. She was married to a big shot man down south. They had one boy when they lived back there. Her husband was killed in a bad car crash, so Phyliss moved herself and her son north. It wasn't long before she married another big shot man in the little town we all lived in.

Her new man, Al, wasn't southern or a looker. He was a big shot northerner with money. They quarreled all the time. Phyliss didn't mind. She told Al that she was good enough for him and she wasn't going to let him boss her around.

He tried everything, but none of the things he'd been taught about women worked with her. She wouldn't go to church with him. She came into a big bunch of money from her first husband's death, and she kept her own checkbook and didn't have to mind nobody. He didn't get a dime of her money, and she hired a weekly housekeeper to boot.

It was rare back then for a woman to decide what to do with her own money. The rest of us handed our paychecks over to our husbands the minute we got home on pay days. Except Maude. She was a widow. Having an empty hand back in those days from your woman keepin' her money from ya', kept Al in a rage, even though he plenty of his own. Phyliss shrugged him off and sallied forth and laughed at what she called Al's "silliness."

Phyliss and Wanda coordinated the food they brought to our dinner. Wanda brought green beans boiled with ham hocks. Phyliss wasn't much of a cook, so she brought a big apple pie she'd purchased at the grocery store and baked at home. She'd shook extra cinnamon on it to make it more homey. We were anxious to try it; frozen apple pies were a brand new product on the market back then. Only big shots would ever think of buying one readymade. It tasted like frozen apple pie baked in a cardboard double crust with some extra cinnamon on it. I eat a piece and didn't say one word for or against. I didn't ask for seconds, though I admired her daring.

Wanda was the baby of their big family. She was the kid sister everybody wanted. But she was married to a mean and stupid man. They had two kids. The boy was just like him, and the girl was just like her. We all knew Wanda was one of those smart women who played dumb to keep her husband thinkin' he was way smarter than her. That's the way many women had to handle men back then. I guess after a while, Wanda got to believin' it, him making fun of her all the time ever' where, in front of the kids, outside the church on Sundays, in the grocery store, didn't matter where.

We none liked her man. He was one of them tall, thin men with a caved in chest and hips that stuck out. He sure was ugly, and Wanda was as pretty as could be. I never did hear how they got together. Didn't want to, 'cause it might be the same as my story. Her man worked at the car parts factory too, and he liked to come up to our floor, swagger around, and scol Wanda in front of us.

We hid what we thought of him and treated him like he was decent in front of her 'cause we didn't want to hurt her. We'd tell him to go to hell if it was left up to us, if we didn't give a damn about Wanda.

Well, we finally fixed her ol' man up. We got our chance one day when Wanda was off sick. He come up to the third floor, struttin' around, building up a head of steam, figurin' to flirt with us. Boy, did we ever give him hell! We made fun of him and scoffed at every word he said, and told him in plain words exactly what we thought of him. We told him we was gonna' do everything we could to help Wanda leave his sorry ass. He left in a hurry with us laughin' behind him.

He stayed away after that and only come up to the third floor when he had real business with Wanda. He never stopped by where we worked again.

We could see Wanda was wonderin' why he didn't come by and scold her any more in front of us, but she never asked, and we sure as hell didn't tell. After awhile, she talked a couple of times about the "duty" she owed him because she was married to him, and she had to endure because there were kids to raise now. She'd figured out by that time that we didn't like him any more than she did.

Every one of us girls working on the third floor of that old car parts factory was from the same old southern place except for Margie. She was from Nebraska. That was a world away from anything we knew of. Margie was short and heavy and pretty. She called it corn fed. She laughed all the time, and it sounded like water bubblin' over a waterfall. She'd make you think of a ripe peach with her big head of curly red hair and her fuzzy pink skin.

Margie's mind never left her man and their four boys. Her man was way too handsome for his own good. Most of the time she was the only one holdin' down a job. She paid for everything and waited on him and their four boys hand and foot at home. None of them lifted a finger to cook or clean or do anything. She mowed the lawn with a push mower her man bought second-hand for her to mow with.

Margie would come in to work cryin' over him borrowing money in her name without askin' her. She was already making their house payments. He bought himself a jeep. She made the payments. He bought a boat. She paid. A big fine barbeque grill, and on and on. He always told whoever he bought somethin' from that she was good for the money. He kept charming her out of it, and she kept letting him get away with it.

I guess she finally had enough, for she started seein' another man. We didn't like her running around, so we scolded her. She scolded us back right quick.

"Yeah. You've all got such great marriages, right? Last night my husband bragged to my face that I'm his meal ticket, his own little sugar mama, and I can't do a damn thing about it."

She told us plenty more once she got started. We shut our mouths real quick. We hugged her and told her to go ahead, she had our backing before she told us too much about our own lousy marriages. We watched and saw that running around with another man and us backing her up made her able to stand up to her husband and four lazy sons.

Margie never did leave that gold digger, but things got straightened out at home real fast. He got a job and kept it. The boys started doing chores. Margie started a checking account and a secret savings account. She came into work smilin' and hummin' again.

Three men worked up on the third floor. Red Bill, Gary, and Jim. Red Bill brought the car parts to us. Gary kept our machines running and lifted the parts for us. Jim came up once in a while to fix a machine or set up a new one. Jim was the only one from back home. Gary and Red Bill were from little towns close to the factory. We liked Red Bill and Gary. None of us liked Jim.

Red Bill was a red haired middle aged hippie with a ponytail hanging down past his waist. He was short and wide and stout and rode a motorcycle to work. His slim, tall wife looked just like Olive Oil. They had fourteen kids, adopted and otherwise, and owned a little purple house in a little town a few miles away. Red Bill was educated, but he only talked it once in awhile. That man was happy all the time.

One time me and Wanda was lookin' out the window watchin' the snow fall. Red Bill drove by on his fork lift. He thowed' his arms out wide and yelled in his big booming voice, "Ahhh, solidified precipitation!"

Gary repaired our machines and carried stock for us. He was a middle-aged man who suffered greatly from the wrong kind of wifely attention. He told us about his wife and daughter while he fixed machines or stacked car parts. He said the blood runnin' in him demanded heat and passion, but his wife Stella was dull as January, and cold as a stone.

He said he stuck with her because they both got a late start in life. Then they had a baby girl, and he knew she'd be in peril if he left. He'd look off somewhere, then sigh and say, "I've accepted my Fate."

No matter how much he complained about Stella, he never mentioned her looks. Gary was handsome, with a pirates build, dark hair, and sparkling black eyes. We'd all seen Stella. Not to be mean, but we figured she coulda' won every ugly contest in the state and maybe the tri-state area 'cause of her attitude and sour face.

She wouldn't get a job. She stayed home, but she never turned a hand. She wouldn't clean house or cook. She wouldn't do laundry or dust. She wore ugly clothes and rollers in her hair all day. Gary did everything at home while she read magazines or watched television. Once in awhile, he brought us pumpkin or zucchini bread. It was always perfect and delicious.

Stella drove him crazy. She gave him a new set of rules to obey each day before he went to work. The rules were all about keeping him from finding someone else he might like a whole lot better than her.

÷

Jim was tall and spare and thought he was the finest man in town. He told us over and over how smart and thrifty he was, and how lucky his wife was because he chose her. Jim admired himself for being a practical man. He measured up to all of the standards of the day. He owned property. He went to church on Sundays. His wife was obedient to him and thrifty, not spending all of his hard earned money. Their son was the spitting image of Jim. Jim was a fine handyman around the house, he always carried cash in his pocket, and every three years he bought a new car and paid cash for it.

But Jim was empty inside, and always mad about it and blaming someone else. We could see the desperation gathering strength in his eyes. That's when he offered to buy us coffee out of the vending machine while he sneaked in a painful pinch somewhere on us. I liked coffee back then, before it gave me a galloping heart, so I got more than my share of black and blue marks before I learned to stay out of his way. He was always after me because I was the youngest woman working up on the third floor. I was the kid in a bunch of women old as my mother and older.

Jim's son was older than me, but that didn't stop Jim. Jim and the men working downstairs in that factory acted like dogs in heat, always sneakin' after or lying about the nice family women working on the first and second floors. Most were the ages of the women I worked with every day. Older women who had to make a living. Fine, good natured women with kids close to my age. Women that kept their heads down and their hands full of work while most of their men swaggered around waggling you know what.

I'd been the kid downstairs at the factory. It didn't take me long to beg the foreman to get transferred up to the third floor where a handful of women worked, and just three men. Somebody took pity on me, for I had to work, and couldn't quit. I got transferred up there, and relief was the main word.

Well, that's the five women I worked with all them years ago, when I wasn't much more than a girl, and didn't have any place or anyone to take my troubles to. I worked with them women for over ten years.

I was the youngest and Old Maude was at the other end of the bunch. Janel, Phyliss, Wanda, and Margie was all in their late thirties or early forties. Somewhere in there. I was in my early twenties. I'd made the worst mistake I'd ever make by marryin' a bad man, a monster. I dreaded goin' home every day to him 'cept I had a little girl so I had to work and go home to him for her sake.

I took my girl and quit him for good while I still worked up on the third floor in the car parts factory. Those five women stood right by me while my family turned the other way. Some of them sided with him, and I'm old now, but I never forgot which ones done that to me.

I made it back then, in spite of all the bad things that went on, and I made it mostly because of them good women and those couple of good guys working at the car parts factory.

The monster wouldn't leave us alone. He kept us scared and living in hell every day and night. So I grabbed a good man I met in the car parts factory and married him quick in self-defense. In a couple years, we moved out of state and started over.

All of that happened after this Thanksgiving dinner I'm tellin' you about.

Red Bill and Gary, Old Maude, Phyliss, Janel, Wanda, Margie and me set down at the table. That old blue canner filled with boiled down tom turkey set in the center of the table. We laughed and talked and then it come time to say a blessing over the food. We all looked at the good food on the table and then at each other. All the words we never said to each other stood in our eyes. We knew deep in our bones and hearts and blood that we wished each other well. It went that deep. We held hands and dropped our heads and said thank you to God like we was supposed to, but we meant each other and all of us knew it.

That was the first time I tasted turkey better than any my Mom ever made. An old boiled down mean assed tom turkey Maude wasn't afraid of dealin' with.

That was the Thanksgiving dinner I got the guts to push past where Mom stopped with her man. Me and my girl could go past both of em'. I became able to do it 'cause that handful of good women and those two good men pushed me along like a baby red tailed hawk—a tough, common ol' bird back where we come from.

When I succeeded and moved away, I carried the memories of those years and that Thanksgiving dinner at the car parts factory with me. That old factory closed a long time ago, almost too far back for anyone to remember. But I will always remember the unforgettable acts of kindness we gifted each other with.

7.   Charlie's Big Fish Story

The names of the people involved in this fish tale were changed to protect the innocent. Most fish tales are famous for being tall tales. A big pack of lies based on a tiny truth. But this fish tale is true. It really happened. How do I know? Because it happened to my cousin Ross, a teller of tall tales and a happy go lucky lady's man.

It started early one morning when I was at work. My boss was out of town. The door was propped open to let the spring breeze in. All was quiet, and I was doing unimportant paperwork when the clock struck ten. Just then my cousin Ross raced through the office door. He ran to my desk and slid to a stop on his knees in front of my office chair. I sat back, grinning. I'd warned him before about rug burns. He grabbed my hands in his, laid his head on them and started sobbing. Please don't feel sorry for him or shocked. He's very emotional, so I have to warn you, this has happened before. Most of our lives, in fact.

÷

Ross takes after the Weber branch of our family, the side yearning to go on the stage. Like them, he's silver tongued and almost as wordy as Grandpa Weber was. Ross is six feet tall. He is well built with bronzed skin, a mane of brown hair and twinkling brown eyes. Good natured, he is in excellent health and exudes endless vitality. His thin, quirky mouth stays in a smile. Ross blabs his guts out to the world and he loves nothing better than a joke. He can sing or shout or get mad or cry instantly, and he never met a stranger. Yep, that's the Weber side for you.

An endless supply of women adore him. They call him tall, handsome, emotional, poetic, romantic and spontaneous while he just looks smug. Ross is forever caught up in a moral dilemma involving a woman he knew, just met, or picked up somewhere. Women tend to drop him notes while he's eating crawdads, his favorite food.

Ross tries his best to meet the standards of the church he grew up in and mind his mother's straight laced teachings, but he fails miserably. He can't avoid the temptation of women. He loves them all, married, single, available, not available, from the tiniest tot to the oldest, wrinkled, prune faced hag.

Temptation always hunts Ross down. Women are drawn to him like moths to a flame. Except he's never killed any of them with his flame, although things get quite toasty at times!

His not so shady and shady ladies show up and leave like traffic passing through a revolving door in a busy department store. From the end of his first romance, which started as soon as he could speak, and up to today, he brings the stories to me.

I've listened to loud, dramatic sessions of self-loathing, recriminations and sins, hell's fire and brimstone, and his fears of a vengeful, long suffering God catching up with him. This symbiosis has gone on since we were children.

÷

I readied myself to listen to another desperate drama of love lost or won, but this time, his dire predicament didn't involve a woman. It involved a fish, the men he works with at the advertising agency, and Charlie, his boss.

Ross climbed to his feet and paced the floor. I watched his expressive face change with emotions. He began his story with large sweeps of his arms. I was glad my office was a big room.

÷

"I work out of an open cubicle next to Charlie's office. Charlie's the president of our advertising agency. He's a quiet, dry man completely devoid of a sense of humor. He isn't creative or funny the way an advertising man usually is."

Ross hesitated, then admitted, "We're not proud of it, but we've always made fun of him after work when we go out together. I mean, I've been there seven years and nobody knew anything about him until recently, when all hell broke loose over a fish!

Charlie can't take a joke, and he doesn't think anything us advertising drudges do is funny. The worst is the Friday afternoon staff meetings when he calls us by the wrong name and humiliates us, using the excuse that it is necessary for him to push us into meeting our deadlines.

The only bright spot in working for Charlie,

65

the only benefit of his ornery nature we can find, is that he has a surefire way of keeping our collective creative genius from going off on too many tangents, and never getting our jobs done.”

Ross looked around. I handed him the glass of water I kept on my desk. He downed it in one long swallow, and set the glass back on my desk.

“Charlie's office is sort of like a big, white cake box setting in the middle of the building our offices are in.”

Ross made a box shape with his hands. I nodded.

“Charlie’s office has glass windows on all four sides. The windows have blinds on them he closes for privacy when meeting with clients. The rest of us work out of cubicles surrounding Charlie’s office. There are fifteen of us, and we are all pals. We know each other’s histories, and we go out pretty often together.”

÷

Ross said Charlie came into work one day looking extremely upset. Ross wondered what happened, but since Charlie never talked to them about anything but work, he didn’t ask.

A short time later, Charlie called Ross into his office. He locked the door and closed the blinds. Then he turned to Ross and tried to speak, his mouth working like a gasping fish, but couldn't. He rushed to his desk, fell into his chair, laid his head on the desk, then started pounding the desktop with his fists.

It all happened so fast that Ross just stood there, dumbfounded. Then Charlie jumped up and started pacing the floor. Ross watched him pace back and forth like he was observing a tennis match. Then Charlie erupted.

"Someone stole my fish!"

Ross watched him uneasily, wondering if Charlie had lost his mind. Two nickels short of a quarter. Finally Charlie explained that he'd gone on a fishing trip with his father a few months ago. It was the last thing they did together before his father suddenly died of a heart attack.

During the fishing trip, Charlie hooked a big fish and brought it in with his father's help. They'd never helped each other before. Bringing in the fish together broke the ice between them, and they talked about real things for the first time in years and made up some grievances with each other. Charlie had never been so happy.

Charlie took the fish home and put it in his freezer, planning to cook it for his father and himself the next time they got together. Then his father died unexpectedly. For the first couple months, Charlie helped his mother with the funeral and the will and so on, until she was settled in and doing okay again.

Then Charlie remembered the fish. He decided to take it to a taxidermist and have it stuffed and mounted. He would hang it on a wall in his den. Then he'd always have a good memory to look at.

Charlie dropped the fish off at the taxidermist, but when he went back to pick the fish up, the taxidermist said the fish was already gone. He gave it to a guy who came in and said he was picking it up for Charlie.

Charlie argued with the taxidermist, but it didn't do any good. He made the taxidermist describe the guy who picked up the fish, but the description could have fit many different men.

Charlie said he came straight to the office because he just had to have someone to talk to about the fish. He said he chose Ross because he knew he could trust him to keep his mouth shut. Ross was astonished. Charlie was so closed-mouthed, no one at the agency knew his father had passed away!

Ross said he comforted Charlie as best he could. Charlie finally calmed down. Before he left Charlie's office, Ross promised to keep Charlie's secret. He backed carefully out of Charlie's office, gingerly shut Charlie's office door, and rushed back to his desk in relief.

The week passed and it came time for the Friday afternoon staff meeting. By then, Ross could see that Charlie was becoming suspicious of the advertising guys. Ross could tell he was thinking that any one of them could have stolen his precious fish. Charlie was harsher than ever during the meeting.

First thing Monday morning, Charlie called Ross into his office again. He bolted the door and lowered the blinds again. Then he shoved a long white envelope into Ross's hand and said, "There is no Bass Place or Albacore Garden in this entire city!"

Ross wondered again if Charlie was a load short of a fish chip. Fried of baked. That might become the question. On the envelope was spelled out "Special Delivery" in large black marker. Ross opened it. Inside was a single sheet of white paper. It was a ransom note. The crude letters on the note were cut from parts of a newspaper and pasted onto the paper. He read the ransom note.

"If you ever want to see your fish again, bring $10,000 in coins- toss in fountain corner of Bass Place & Albacore Garden midnight tonight. Come alone."

Ross's first instinct was to burst out laughing. With an effort worthy of that old time famous actor Lionel Barrymore, whom the Weber side of our family admired greatly, he managed to control himself. He kept his face blank, but shining with empathy while Charlie paced the floor and ranted.

Ross sympathized with him and got out of Charlie's office as quick as he could. He hurried back to his desk and tried to concentrate on his work, but the urge to laugh grew like bread batter when the yeast is truly working; it kept rising and rising and rising inside him. It kept growing until he knew he was going to burst if he didn't let it out. He rushed to the bathroom and hooted with laughter between bouts of gut wrenching sympathy for Charlie.

Then Joe, one of the guys he worked with, walked in. Joe grinned at him and nodded. He seemed to know what Ross was laughing about.

Ross blurted out how badly Charlie was taking their joke and why. He told Joe they should return the stolen fish. Joe apologized. He explained to Ross that they intended it as a joke. They didn't know what the fish really meant to Charlie when they stole it. Now that they knew, they would give the fish back. Joe asked Ross not to tell Charlie on them, or they might lose their jobs. Ross promised not to tell.

A couple hours later, Charlie called an unscheduled staff meeting. He fumed and paced and ranted about their work not being up to par. He was unreasonable with all of them, including Ross. The guys looked at each other and an unspoken agreement ran between them. The fish was not to be returned. Ross asked them not to share any fish plans with him. They agreed. Charlie stayed unreasonable in the staff meetings; the result was more ransom notes about the fish.

Charlie didn't let up, so the guys got tougher. Polaroid pictures were sent. Charlie called Ross into his office again and handed him a Polaroid snapshot of the fish. It was standing on its tail in beach sand. It wore sunglasses with a hula skirt around its waist. A tube of coconut oil lay beside it on the beach. In the background was a blue sky. A sign stuck in the sand read, "Having fun in Acapulco! Wish you were here!"

It took all Ross could do to keep from laughing outright. After he calmed Charlie down, he rushed to the bathroom and laughed and cried again.

Another staff meeting, another Polaroid of the fish was sent. In it, the fish wore a small cowboy hat and spurs on its fins. It was dangling from a hangman's noose. In the background was a "Boot Hill" sign with tiny wooden crosses bearing names such as Molly Flounder, Jack Mackerel, and Luke Lutefisk. Another meeting, and the next Polaroid arrived. The fish was laid out on a fish plate beside a microwave oven with salt, pepper, lemon, a fork, knife, and drawn butter beside the plate.

But the fish didn't get eaten. It was sent to an ashram instead to save it from the unholy fate of being eaten. With its life intact, the fish took up golf. A Polaroid came showing the fish setting out on an extended golf tour. It stood by a tiny set of golf clubs, wearing a checkered tam on its head. The fish toured Europe. It became a matador with a tri-corner hat holding a red cape in Spain. In Japan, the fish became a Samurai with a long pigtail and tiny swords. In Sweden, it did its genealogy and learned that it was related to Luke Lutefisk.

The fish returned from Europe. Charlie received a Polaroid of his fish with a sign in the background reading, "America or Bust!"

The fish returned home, settled down and got married. Charlie received a picture of the wedding. His fish wore a tuxedo. It was standing in front of a miniature church. The bride to be was smaller and posed beside Charlie's fish. She wore a petite white veil because she was a whitefish. Of course, her name was Pearl. Pearl Whitefish. Later, pictures came of two little sun fish standing beside them, one poached and one baked.

Charlie's fish ran for President. Then he became a cowboy and moved his family west in a covered wagon. His wife and daughter wore sunbonnets while he and his son wore tiny ten gallon Stetsons.

Each time Charlie received another picture of the fish, he called Ross into his office and ranted. The situation worsened. Charlie was becoming almost demented with his fish problem. He began receiving anonymous food deliveries from every fish place in town. The fish came boiled, fried, baked, poached, grilled, and extra crispy with tartar sauce, all C.O.D.

÷

By that time, under all the pressure from Charlie, and aware of what his pals were up to, Ross took up talking to himself. His love life was suffering for the first time. He forgot to pay his bills or put gas in his car or eat crawdads. He often left his house for work in his fleece leisure pants with the Florida Marlins' fish logo on them, or the Miami Dolphins, depending on his laundry status and what fish story he'd just heard from Charlie.

As Ross told me all this, I felt his pain, and nixed my plan to have shrimp salad for lunch.

"I can't stand it anymore, and that's why I'm here." he said. "What am I going to do?"

Briskly I said, "Simple. Give the guys an ultimatum. Tell them to return the fish immediately, or else!"

Ross stared at me a minute. "Or else what?"

"Who knows? Let them figure it out."

"That simple, huh?" he said.

"Yes," I answered crisply.

Ross went back to work and gave the guys an ultimatum. Return the fish to Charlie immediately, so he could keep his sanity, or else!

He told me later that everything worked out well. The guys were starting to feel bad about the fish situation, so they sent Charlie a final ransom note with a key to a locker at the old bus station downtown.

Charlie rushed downtown and opened the locker. He pulled his fish out of the locker and examined it closely. But this fish was not the same fish he'd caught on the trip with his father! He was stunned. His shoulders slumped in despair. He shook his head disconsolately. Would this damned fish story never end? Would poached, baked, boiled, fricasseed and fried fish flavor every day of his life forever?

He took the fish home and put it in the freezer in the same spot where he once placed the original fish. Then he went back to work and never said a word to the guys about it being the wrong fish.

But something was on Charlie's mind, and whatever it was made him so absent-minded that he became milder and more forgiving of the guys methods and mistakes.

Time passed. The guys thought the ordeal was over. They were sitting around sneaking yawns and being bored while listening to Charlie during a Friday afternoon staff meeting.

Suddenly Charlie reached into a large paper bag, pulled out the fish, and held it up for the guys to see. None of them knew what to do, so they all grinned hugely and applauded him, hoping they wouldn't get fired.

Charlie said, "This is NOT the same fish I caught on the fishing trip with my father!"

Looks of surprise flashed over their faces.

Charlie said, "When I found the wrong fish in the bus station locker, I started wondering what the hell my father was up to. What was he trying to tell me? I asked this because this fish situation has kept my relationship with him stirred up and right in my face. So it had to be his doing, god bless his fishy, shrimp eating soul!

Then I asked myself, "What if my father somehow knew he was going to die, and we still hadn't worked out our differences? What if he, in some sort of strange way—who knows how things really work?—picked you guys to help him get through to me by having you steal the fish?"

The guys looked at each other. Was this really Charlie speaking? Or was he an imposter, like the fish? And where was the real fish? Who took it?

Then Charlie said he knew they'd always wanted him to be more human and reasonable and at least remember their names. He said he wanted the same thing from his father and felt he only achieved it once, and that was on their last fishing trip. Charlie grinned at Ross and the guys.

"And if you guys hadn't stole the fish and put me through living fish hell, my own son might have grown up like I did, and the chance for me to be a better father would have passed. I now believe that's what my father wanted me to learn. Now I read the funnies to my son on Sunday mornings, and we laugh together and go fishing."

He concluded, "So on behalf of my father, that prankster and big fish story teller now living in the Great Fishing Ground in the Sky, thank you guys for stealing the fish from me. In its place I gained something much more important."

Silence filled the room. All the guys were sons of somebody and some of them were fathers. They teared up. They were a part of what was supposed to be a joke, but what turned out to be the longest ordeal they'd ever suffered through. It was obvious the whole thing had made them better men than they were before. Were they heroes of some kind now? Who the heck knew?

Charlie strolled past them and shut the door to the meeting room behind him. They sat in solemn silence for a minute. Then they all started talking at once. Ross asked how they knew about Charlie's fish. It turned out that one of the guys was related to the taxidermist, who mentioned Charlie's fish at a family gathering. Ralph had Jason, someone the taxidermist didn't know, pick up the fish. No one ever knew where the real fish disappeared to. Jason put Charlie's fish in the locker for Charlie to find, and he did. That's all he knew.

÷

Ross started to leave after telling me the end of his fish story a few weeks later. He was wearing tan slacks and white shirt instead of his Marlin sweats. I ran after him and asked if he wanted to join me for lunch.

He said "Sure. A shrimp salad would go down real good!...or crawdads!"

No one ever found out what happened to the real fish Charlie caught on the trip with his father. Ross eventually moved on to another job. Before he left, he said Charlie gave him a journal. The title on the cover was "Fish Fry on Sundays-A Fisherman's Guide to the Universe."

8.   The Seer's Cottage

The Seer lived in an ancient, two story frame cottage with a rickety, once upon a time, white picket fence wandering drunkenly around her weed, flower, and vegetable choked front yard. To my eyes, this was haphazard nonsense. Who else planted vegetables in their front yard? Nobody, that's who. I waited each time I passed by her place to be filled with disapproval like my mother would have been if she saw this mess, and to not give the Seer a second thought; that's what mother would have expected.

But true to my secret, escapist nature, I was filled with delightful, unexplainable contentment each time I passed by the Seer's cottage. I knew the cause was the magic of the drunken fence and crooked lines painted on the sides of her place. My mother said I was unexplainable and filled with forbidden curiosity. That caused her to forever call me "odd" and dismiss me with frequent frowns.

I discovered the Seer's cottage because of mother-condemned curiosity. In my childhood, the boredom from the hollow, exacting, everlasting routine my grim and unsympathetic mother laid out for every spare inch of my life caused me to soon get in the habit of rebelling any way I could, at least for short minutes, as quickly as I got out of her sight.

The Seer's drunken fence and wandering paint job contented me. Her flowers did too. They grew here and there with no plan. I guess everything else about her place, especially the fact that she was a Seer, fascinated me. Seers knew magic. I didn't know what kind, but they practiced magic. No one else I knew did. I knew she was a Seer too, because the sign hanging by her front door said so.

I discovered the Seer's cottage on a detour to the dreaded, boring, elementary school I attended, where I was too thin and too little to take up for myself with anybody. That was true at home and everywhere else, too. I was ignored as though I didn't exist, as though solemn, pale little girls with straight brown hair didn't matter. I hated school and got there as late as I dared, but never told mother.

I never went far out of the way, for I might end up late for school, and my mother would punish me with mean words when I got home. I had a great imagination as a child. Mother had none. Later in life, I realized that her lack of imagination was the thing that kept me scared as a rabbit for all those years before she died. Until then, I stayed frozen. Bored, frightened, and lackluster.

My eyes wandered over the Seer's cottage until they rested on the fence. Morning dew stood in tear drops on tan roses crowded against the wandering wood. The roses pushed through the crooked slats as if to find me, scenting the air with a beckoning air hinting of the mysteries of a bygone era folded within them. At the time, I didn't know the tan roses were ancestral roses, saved over several centuries of time, replanted again and again. I looked at the tears on them. They matched the forever tears that stood still, but sometimes ran through places in me. Forbidden emotional places that my tiny, grim, dragon mother guarded against.

"No tears! Never!" She scolded me in a rough, loud voice when I was a baby, until the day came when I understood what was to be. I stopped crying outside and held it inside where I wept steadily through the days of my childhood, tears hidden from sight or sound.

Mother's disapproval of me was the only sound that broke the dull silence in our house. Sometimes I did things just to hear something, anything louder than the dull, low voices of my mother and father stating only what was necessary for survival.

The Seer's cottage sat a dozen yards back from the broken gray sidewalk meandering through the forgotten neighborhood it was a part of. Her small, peaked cottage was painted the same haphazard white as the fence. I just knew the Seer painted the fence and walls while she was day dreaming. I knew this because she gave them the same kind of paint job I imagined would have.

In the beginning, the first time I saw it, the cottage looked crazy to me with snow white drunken stripes from her paint roller covering it here and there. But as the days went by, it started looking sort of nice. Sort of like there was a pattern to it. Like it was trying to say something, but couldn't get the right words out.

Like me.

Each day the sun dappled the Seers paint job into different patterns and secret messages, moving the shadows cast by the tall trees and overgrown bushes surrounding the cottage to different places on its daily trek across the heavens.

I gave up my other detours. I studied the messages in her paint job each time I passed her place on my way to school. After giving much thought to the matter, I decided the Seer owned a spontaneous, artistic inner system. One she pursued life with. This deduction pleased me by making her even more mysterious.

Time passed. After a while, I could see that the paint job was part of her alphabet for coping with life. I knew because I already had a few coping methods of my own in the experimental stages. Developmental codes. Maybe she'd entered some kind of code in the lines that might be seen from on high, maybe by an airplane? Or an angel? Like "SOS", or "HELP!"

Even though I never saw the Seer, I already knew she was different than anyone I would ever meet. Not for her the perfection of a neat paint by numbers job to please everyone else, like I would have done because I was supposed to.

I studied the warp and weave in the drunken lines of house paint and decided that an everyday, hum drum life was not for the Seer. No. She was a bold old woman who did what I wasn't able to do so far, and probably never would; she boldly came forth with a language that told whatever it was that was going on with her to whoever without apology, even if was through drunken lines that nobody else understood the words to.

My mother forever said I was odd because I simmered like a stopped up sieve when I got around old houses with good "bones" or any place where "artsy stuff" was, as she called it. She didn't like that her only child was odd and a girl, too. A grinning, stout, silent boy would have been my father's responsibility to shape into a strong, silent fisherman, and she would have been off the hook for it if the boy behaved badly.

But no, all she had was me, and I wasn't much, as she often said. She took exception to my odd "simmering", and ordered me to save it for church, a place where it mattered. From then on, I simmered behind her back and grew even more morose and silent and proper in front of her and my father and the dismal church goers. Yes, I was a quick learner in some ways. Not many. Just enough to duck and dodge and get by on.

I gave the Seer and her paint job some thought every day on the detour I took past her place on my way to my dull school, where I stayed a silent, unseen student with a "C" average. I turned my thoughts to the Seer when the other students made fun of me because I didn't want to be popular. Yakking all the time sapped my innards; it cost too much in both words and connections; it took my breath away. I knew all about innards because of watching my father clean the fish he caught. Those bratty kids didn't understand me any better than I understood them or the Seer, so we stayed even while wandering through the great halls of learning.

Mother and I were neither one big talkers or deep thinkers, although we both read newspapers, books, whatever we could get our hands on, with the exception of what she labeled "smut," which meant no silly romances, no silly nonsense like C.S. Lewis or Tolkien. We kept a steady routine with staid, sedate books that told a person what to do and what to think; that was the way of it.

Both my father and mother came from a long line of silent, morose fishing families who docked at the wharves downtown and sold their days catch there before wearily trudging home to soup and silence. The whole bunch believed that silence was not only golden, it was holy. Silence was wise. Silence was proper and noise was ill advised. Music was out of the question. Any kind. Their world stayed insistently gray, foggy, and misty, allowing no mystery or color to it.

Since no one ever asked them any questions, I never knew if they knew anything. Their rock solid, silent opinions matched the church and their politics. They could quell a rebellion without a word, with just a look or a squint.

I asked my father once if the ocean was noisy. He gave me a long look and asked me why. "Maybe that's why you like silence so much." He looked away and didn't answer. I knew I wouldn't get an answer before I asked the question. I didn't like the sea. The sea was loud and noisy and full of movement that gave me vertigo and made me seasick, but not father. It talked to him in ways I never could.

I never told anyone about the Seer's cottage.

It was my own secret. None of them would have cared anyway. Everyone I knew, which happened to be just a handful of people, wanted life to be silent with as few words as possible in it. They needed total predictability without a question interrupting that holy process. No bumps allowed in the road. So I kept my mouth shut.

But when it rained, I walked by her cottage to listen and watch how the house and yard and picket fence changed when it was wet. I went back to listen and watch the snow falling on everything. I went back again to listen to the fall wind gusting around the eaves, and in the middle of the hot, still summer to admire the bold red poppies planted by her gate blooming loud and careless. Watching the Seers cottage spoke to the lonesome, needy part of me that forever yearned for beauty and words, and gave it rest.

I took up watching the Seer's cottage from the vacant lot across the street while hours passed and cotton-colored stripes slowly took over the empty spots where the sun touched the walls on its journey across the sky. I watched and munched on tuna sandwiches and drank water from a stolen milk bottle while the flowers and bushes grew and covered the rest of the wood until the unpainted parts didn't show any more.

By then, I knew the different scents of the Seers flowers and weeds, and I'd seen her outside more than once. She was older than anyone I would ever meet; I just knew it. She hobbled along like the oldest fisherman down at the wharf. She was bent and wrinkled and wore a scarlet handkerchief tied around her bushy white hair. I ran away each time I saw her, even though she seemed to pay no attention to me.

÷

I grew up and the Seer's cottage grew older. My father died of a heart attack while fishing out on the river the spring I graduated from high school. It was a predictable ending for him. Just my mother and I were left now. We were the last of both branches of our family.

My mother expected me to marry straight out of high school. I was to marry a fisherman, too. But I made other plans, even though ingrained in me were family genetics urging me towards living out a life of predictability. Genetics would always have a strong place in my life. They would limit me as to speech and most likely any changes I ever thought about making. I knew that, and accepted the situation for what it was. No firebrands in our heritage. No change makers or trailblazers. That fact didn't bother me. I only expected to go so far anyway; I just hoped to go at least a little ways.

I got a job in the city in a large department store and began to commute back and forth every day. It took me awhile to learn how to get there and back, but I was tenacious, so I learned it.

The department store liked that I was plain and stayed soft spoken with few words and didn't volunteer opinions. I would never make a manager; I never wanted to, for they needed to have the gift of gab. I was the perfect sales girl

84

and knew it. I got to handle rich clothing and revel in all the colors and scents of the different kinds of beauty surrounding me. I should have been more ambitious, but I wasn't. It was enough for me to dream in color, to hope to retire from the department store someday.

Once I was familiar with my commute and my job, I took up my old school detour again, examining the Seer's latest paint job with my eyes to see how it changed each day on my way to work. The faded shingle still hung beside the front door of her deep, wide porch, the hand painted sign announcing that she was a "Seer" and would tell your future for a dime.

I often studied the sign, wondering what the Seer would tell a poor, morose, speechless, plain girl, a department store clerk with no future, who liked old cottages and houses instead of fishing. Who got seasick and laughed at and left behind and was glad of it. Relieved.

÷

It happened early one summer morning when I was on my way to the bus stop. I was standing on the cracked and crooked sidewalk in front of her cottage, shading the sun from my eyes with my hand, staring at the sign when the Seer caught me.

"Hey, you!" she boomed. I squeaked in fright and dropped my purse. I hadn't see her working in the garden pushing its wild, bold way past the rickety picket fence.

"Have you got that dime yet?" she boomed, making her way towards the falling down slats of the faded fence to where I stood on the other side. I hastily grabbed up my purse and dug through it for my change purse.

"Have you found it yet?" her voice echoed loudly through the quiet old neighborhood of mostly small cottages set back from the street. The insistence in her voice didn't fit anything surrounding us.

"I got plenty to tell you. It's time, you know. You been comin' by here for years, a' waitin'. Now it's time."

The flower laden air stayed patient and heavy with morning moisture and the discreet chirping of birds, making the way she disturbed them and caught me seem like a sin. She hobbled the last couple of feet to the fence and stuck out a long, bony hand to take the dime from me. I tossed it into her upturned palm. She grinned a wide, full-toothed smile at me. I barely glanced at her face. I watched her hand. As soon as I saw the dime was safely in her palm, I turned and scurried down the street. I heard her voice booming after me before I turned the corner of the block.

"Hey! Come back! Don't you want to know what I can tell you?"

I heard my genetics shouting back at her. Both mother and father and their lineages were shouting "No!" They were the reason I scurried down the street. I couldn't stop myself, turn around and go back, though I wanted to. The silent weeping inside me started up again.

When I was safely around the corner, the sound of her voice faded. I felt sad but vastly relieved. I thought about her while I smiled and soothed customers, using the power of my inherited silence for the first time with an acute awareness of it. I never knew silence held such power. I had refused the Seer. I did what my lineage approved of. I didn't stray from their path of silence when tempted.

For that reason, I became deathly afraid of the future the Seer might have prophesied for me. I felt relieved and secretly proud for running from a prophesied future that I, no doubt, wouldn't have been able to fulfill. That was the other secret reason. I would have been exploring beyond where my people stopped, and I had no tools to do it with. I couldn't bring myself to try, either. What was, was. I accepted my fate. I was struck silent, and would forever remain that way. I accepted it.

÷

Now that there was only me and mother left of the joint fishing lineages, I planned to be the last one. I didn't want to go any further by marrying and producing just the right amount of children to carry on a heritage that held no beauty, only silent duty.

I knew that whatever kind of man I got, good or bad, I'd let him keep me. I wouldn't be able to leave him because whoever I got, I was going to keep. Having no man at all was better than what the Seer might have prophesied for me. By then, I'd convinced myself that she would have got my hopes up about changing, and I might have taken a bad risk.

87

÷

After that fateful morning, I still detoured by her place each workday, but I started using the sidewalk across the street from it, crossing at the corner to take the bus into the city. I stayed close, but far enough away so I was safe. I told myself the same story each time I passed near the Seer's cottage so I could go on with my ordinary, safe life.

"I am too shy for this busy world. I am a small, wordless, only child. I live with a grim and tidy mother in a tiny little house at the other end of this place, distant from the Seer and her kind. Mother and I have no other family, just each other and I work as a nameless clerk in a department store downtown, far from this little neighborhood. My life doesn't matter."

Still, every time I took that detour, I wondered what she would have said.

÷

I met Jim about a year after my encounter with the Seer. He worked down at the boatyard and dreamed of owning his own boat business someday. I had no dreams. His brown eyes shone into mine while he told me his dreams in a soft voice, and right then I decided to make them mine. I wanted his dreams more than I wanted him.

Jim was gentle and thoughtful and slow to anger. Best of all, he let everyone around him be just be who they were. He didn't have a problem with people who were different. He followed his own regimen, but didn't need to make anyone else go along with him. I took my time, a couple years of it, to learn Jim. I forgot all about the detour and the old woman who called herself a Seer, who wanted to predict my future. I made my own way. I made Jim's dreams my own.

Jim was a patient, hardworking man and my mother approved of him. When I was ready, we got married. Just as quick as we got married, my mother took sick. We moved in with her and I quit my job so I could take care of her. She wasted away, hanging on forever and another day, wearing me out with her grumbling and griping until she took her last breath on earth a few years later.

Jim and I were both too emotionally exhausted from her negativity to move out of her little house, even though the very walls of it were saturated with her orneriness. We stayed on because she'd left me the house. We cleaned it and built on to it until it was fresh and larger and bore no imprint from her. That took three more years.

Then the children started coming. Four of them. I was an older mother, and more time flew by. I let the children be as noisy as they wanted to be. They grew up and left home. None of them became silent fishermen. They had children of their own, and none of them ever came back.

I remembered them telling me they wanted to live with someone else in some other place where they could shout and cry and laugh all they wanted to, and as often and much as they needed to. They said this place was too gray and dismal for them. I guess I did turn out too much like my parents and their joint fishing lineage after all. Well, as far I was concerned, leaving here was a good success for all of them.

Life flowed by like a smooth stream without a stone blocking it until Jim and I were finally left alone in my mother's empty house. There was nothing I needed to do any more. No children to tend to, no mother to tend to. Jim was retired and healthy, so I set around the house, getting my second wind while he spent each day working on his boat in the garage.

After I rested long enough, my thoughts traveled back in time to the simple, shiny little dime I tossed into the "Seer's" palm. I remembered how it shone in the sunlight, and I wished I'd looked at her face. I wonder once again what she might have seen in me, and what she would have told me about my future that long ago day.

÷

It stayed on my mind until one day I found myself pulling on a fresh pair of pants, an old work shirt and brown shoes to head out for a walk that included an old familiar detour.

The sun was shining. I strolled along. I found myself walking faster, until I was hurrying along. Suddenly I wanted to catch up with that young girl and the old Seer again in the worst way. I wanted to hear every single word she wanted to tell me back then. I needed the Seer's prophecy. I would do whatever she prophesied now. I needed a dream of my own. I just hoped it wasn't too late.

I stopped in front of the Seer's cottage and caught my breath. My eyes swept over the age hollowed emptiness and the good "bones" of the empty cottage, then they went to the large, crooked "For Sale" sign stuck in the front yard, almost covered by tall grass.

She was gone? The Seer was gone? It took me a minute to understand. Of course. She was already old back when I was young. A lot of years had passed since then. Too many for her to live through, probably. A wave of sadness swept over me. I scolded myself in my mother's voice; I was never one to give time much thought.

I looked at the porch. The old sign still hung by the front door. The letters on it were faded and almost gone. What kind of life had she led? Was she in a home or buried somewhere? It looked like I would never know. I came back too late. I was old now, and she was gone. I'd missed my chance.

I leaned against the rickety, dull gray fence. Until this very minute, the secret, reserved, waiting part of me I'd never shared, had believed with no reservation that time would stand still for the Seer and me. I'd be a young girl again, and she'd be an old, wise woman tending her cottage and flowers, and we'd meet again.

Tears tried to gather, but I'd been taught to never cry right from the start of my life, so I resorted to my usual remedy. I went to work.

I studied the fence to keep from further thinking. The flowers and weeds were propping it up. The unkempt yard behind it shouted neglect. It was thick and thirsty with more flowers and shrubs than I remembered. All of them were overgrown. Some were still trying to shove their way through the fence. Bold, undying, pretty things! The scent of flowers and magnolia trees and birds chirping sent me back in time until I became the girl I was the day I tossed the dime in the Seer's palm and scurried away. But this time, I didn't run away.

÷

Without thinking about it, my restless old hands started plucking off the faded buds from the flowers so they would be clean and neat and grow new ones. The work felt good and comforting. I drew in the remembered scent of the tan roses and sighed a long sigh of contentment. I was home.

The sun warmed my back as I worked my way along the falling down fence edge, pulling and plucking, straightening everywhere I could reach. Fixing this. Fixing that. Bringing it back to life. I didn't know what else was coming back to life in the world, but this little part of it needed to be done by me and nobody else.

I worked my way right through the front gate and up the sides of the thin, gray concrete path. The next thing I knew, I was standing on the front porch in front of the door. The doorknob turned easy in my hand. The smell of aged spices and old dust wafted out to greet me. I sniffed. An old, forgotten grief stir inside of me at the scent. I didn't know what it meant, but I couldn't step away from that doorway. I had to go inside.

I stepped into the entry hall, closed the door behind me, and turned around. I thought I would stop there, that I would stare awhile and then go back out the front door, close it behind me, and leave. I knew I was trespassing. But I couldn't leave, and didn't want to. I locked the door behind me, went right on in, and spent hours rambling through the Seers cottage, downstairs and up, through the front and back yard. I talked to myself and sniffled a little the whole time. I examined everything everywhere. I didn't miss a thing inside or out.

I don't remember much of what I said to nobody but me, but I seemed to be listening. I deduced all kinds of things about the absent Seer. Everything I came across defined the Seer to me, and each piece fell into the deep, dreaming place waiting inside me since that day so long ago. It was a place of no criticism, no time, no definitions. Labels and their hard edges were out of the question.

I wanted and needed the Seer and her cottage and her words so I could plant my own dreams and watch them grow. Now, at last, almost too old and too late, I knew. The Seer had wanted to give me the seeds of my dreams for that dime, to pour the seeds of dreams into me that my heritage did not carry and would not allow anyway. Those seeds lay, not in a tall and handsome man, as I once thought, but in words that planted seeds in tall grass that never got mowed.

I was a good person. I had helped my mother's, my husbands, and my children's dreams come true. Now it was my turn.

I went outside and stood on the cracked and broken sidewalk in the old, neglected neighborhood and looked around. Who said this old place was worthless? Who said it wasn't valuable? The homes around here were filled with aged grace. Mosses and ivies and shade trees grew around them. These homes once sheltered many lives and provided many a home base for life to move forward from. The people living in them had grown old, like me. These houses had grown old too, right along with us. I belonged here. I felt it in my bones, and I began to wonder about the exotic, unpredictable Seer's life I once watched from a young, safe place.

Bitter tears burned my eyes and coursed down my face. I never shed a tear since childhood, and didn't know why it was happening now. But it felt good to cry. It didn't bother me none.

I knew I wanted her cottage more than anything else on earth. I never really wanted anything, or planned for a want, not for Jim or my kids or my life. I figured I'd live my life out without one. Like my mother. And my father. But here was my chance.

I hurried back in her cottage to hide from the world in a place I could finally cry myself out in. For once, I was able to let it happen. I smoothed my hands over the walls and door frames of the vestibule and cried. After awhile, the crying stopped. By the time I left the Seer's cottage, my mind was made up. I never owned any dreams of my own. I never had a want so strong I would do anything to satisfy it. No, not one minute of all my life until now.

I blew my nose, wrote down the real estate agent's phone number, walked home and called them.

I had a purpose of my own now, and I meant business. No more giving in to anybody that got in my way. There was a need driving me now like I'd seen happen in movies and to other people and envied. Now it was happening to me. I didn't know what it meant, and didn't care. I'd been freed from something. This time, I would listen to the Seer.

÷

I reasoned it all out before I talked to Jim. We'd put by a tidy little nest egg. I told him I wanted to use the money to buy the Seer's cottage. He was used to me being timid and agreeable, and he couldn't understand why I wanted the cottage. I couldn't put it into words for him.

We always lived our lives the way we, mostly Jim, thought they were supposed to be lived. Jim was kind, and I never objected to him running our show. He never expected me to change. Neither did I.

I stood my ground and worked it out. In the end, I got the Seers cottage, my way. My mother left me the house we lived in free and clear. I earned every inch of it by the time she give up and left this Earth. What was fair, was fair. Jim had a good pension coming in, and our little nest egg didn't have to be touched. I mortgaged my mother's house and used money I'd saved back over the years. It was better that way. Just me paid for the Seer's cottage.

÷

I bought it in the fall, and spent most every day working over there, cleaning the yard and trimming the shrubs; doing the outside work while the weather held. I only went home to cook for Jim and listen to him talk about his boat.

She left behind treasures that would give me a lifelong comfort. In the old shed out back were flowerpots, gardening tools, and a thick gardening journal detailing when and where the Seer planted her flowers.

I carried the worn gardening journal into the kitchen real careful so it wouldn't get any more weather beaten. I placed it on the kitchen table and made myself a cup of tea. I drank it and turned the pages carefully, for I suspected it would become a sacred book to me.

I had been of the rock solid opinion that the Seer was all over the place about everything. But what looked haphazard to me was orderly in a way most people never think about. The Seer understood things I never gave a thought to. Her plants were carefully placed to propagate, to go to seed, and in diligent ways, to help each other live, to blossom or bear fruit.

There was no coffeepot in the Seer's house. Only a teapot, cups and saucers. I kept it that way. No coffee. Coffee was for me and Jim at home. Tea belonged here and only to me after I found her tea set. When I finished my tea ritual, I washed and cleaned and organized everything in the garden shed just the way the Seer's garden journal said to do. Then I planted the fall bulbs. I kept the gardening journal with its notes and drawings hid in the back of a kitchen cupboard. I never took it home with me, not once.

Winter set in. I started the work needed inside the cottage. I watched the snow fall through the windows and took my time wiping down the flowered and striped wallpaper real easy throughout the house, then I re-pasted all the loose strips.

Old books were laying everywhere upstairs. Maybe the Seer used to read at night. I carried them down to the living room, cleaned and organized them, then placed them in orderly rows on the built in book shelves on each side of the fireplace. There were plenty of books and shelves. The books were about anything you could ever think of. Things that never occurred to me. Things that were worth giving a thought to.

I walked to the used store in the little neighborhood and hired them to bring out some small tables and extra bookshelves for the rest of the books.

Everything was dusty. There was one sofa in the house. It was in the living room. It was long with lots of cushions and a high, curved back. When I cleaned it, an old fashioned rose pattern emerged that must have been popular a long time ago. I steam cleaned the rugs. They were the old fashioned kind that wore like cast iron. There were intricate patterns of colorful flowers and bright birds woven into them.

I took down the dusty, heavy drapes from the

windows and carried them to the dry cleaners. They turned out to be dark green with little pink flowers popping out all over them with darker green vines and leaves curling around the flowers. I paced this way and that, admiring them after they were back up.

A gauzy pink material was wound between the posts all the way to the top of the stairs. I wondered what it was put there for, but by now I knew the Seer did everything for a reason. I'd never seen anything like it; I liked the way it looked. I unwound it and hired the stairs and all carpeted areas cleaned. Then I washed the pink material, ironed it, and wound it back through the posts again.

I cleaned the kitchen and washed the few antique dishes and thin, pretty china cups and saucers I'd found in the cupboards. I moved the kitchen table and two chairs to a sunny spot by the back door.

When the kitchen was clean and orderly, I browsed through the little neighborhood stores and found one that carried pretty teapots. I bought a tea set and some of their special teas. I never drank tea as a habit before. Just the bitter black coffee my father and Jim made.

The wonderful names and exotic blends of the teas were all new to me. I pictured myself sitting in one of the kitchen chairs or relaxing before the fireplace in the living room, sipping a cup of tea, inhaling its aroma while reading a book. I would glance out the windows, and there would be snow falling while I sat inside, warm and content by a good fire. Or I could come in after working outside in the spring, carrying the scents of newness in with me while I drank a satisfying cup of tea at the sunny kitchen table.

÷

I saved the Seer's upstairs bedroom for last. The closet still held her clothes. I wondered why she'd left everything. I might never know. By that time, I knew some things. The Seer lived alone in the cottage. There were no signs of children or a husband. There were just enough dishes and everything else for one person. And I knew why, too. Mostly, anyway, because I discovered two more of her journals. One was hidden in the back of a cupboard in the laundry room, the other on top of a bookcase by the fireplace. It was to the back and very dusty.

She left three journals. A gardening journal, a kitchen journal, and a travel journal. That's what I named them.

The kitchen journal was full of exotic, strange old recipes and instructions on how to use the herbs, flowers and weeds she grew for flavoring food and in mendicants. It fit right in with her gardening journal, further explaining why she planted the way she did.

I copied recipes from the kitchen journal, then hid it in the back of the cupboard where I found it. I tried the recipes out at home. I served Jim plantain and sour oranges and deep fried fish with amazing names and exotic fruit desserts. Jim liked them all. He said it made for a change in our routine. He didn't ask any questions, but I told him I got the recipes from the library anyway.

I still couldn't share the Seer's house or journals with him. He knew it, and accepted it and stayed away. Besides, he was busy with his boat and his friends. But sometimes, over the dinner table, we looked each other in the eyes longer than just a quick glance, searching to see what was new in there. But we never went any further.

÷

The Seer's travel journal was filled with photographs of exotic places. The Seer was a world traveler in her younger days. She'd seen the Pyramids in Egypt, and lions in Africa. She went on cruises to Alaska and visited France.

I wondered how she got from there to here, to living out her life in an old neglected neighborhood. Maybe this was her safe place, a place to practice her "eccentric" ways without harm? Everyone living here ignored each other; most were too old or too close to dead to give a damn what anyone else did.

÷

One morning I carried the travel journal upstairs with me, laid it on her bed, and looked around. It was time to take care of her bedroom. I pulled up the shade and opened the window to let the warm air in. I cleaned and washed and dusted while sunshine poured through the window and across her big double bed. The wood plank floor turned gold in the sunlight and the air filled with dancing motes of pollen from the flowering yard below. The long, oval, wood framed mirror on one wall reflected the sunshine.

I opened her closet door and took the Seers clothes out, one at a time, and laid them out on the bed. Mixed in with utility and duty clothes were silky, flowing, colorful pieces, blouses and skirts and dresses. Lovely, costly curves resting on expensive cloth hangers.

I almost stopped and put them back, but reminded myself that I was practiced in handling beautiful clothes from my job in the department store years ago. I sorted out the utility clothes, stacked them, and laid them aside. Then I held up each piece of exotic clothing and examined it carefully as though it was a colorful, thousand year old dream that could dissolve any minute. I studied each shape and stroked the textures with my fingertips, rejoicing in the rich, bright colors as I laid them out on the bed. They would need to be dry cleaned or hand washed. I sorted them into two batches.

When I was done, I turned back to the closet. Beneath the clothes stood a set of expensive caramel colored leather luggage. There were stickers from all over the world pasted on them. I pulled each piece out and set it aside.

Behind the luggage were shoe boxes, neat rows of them stacked against the back closet wall. I knelt down and pulled them out.

The first shoe box was filled with photos from a bygone era, a time when lovely women wore wonderful, long, hanging tube dresses and smart shoes, and handsome men wore Panama hats and white linen suits and posed with curved canes. I studied the pictures closely, but couldn't find the Seer in them.

The second shoe box held a pair of dark purple leather sandals. I took them out and sniffed the soft leather and studied the Italian label. They were barely worn. I laid them aside and opened the rest of the shoe boxes. The next thing I knew, I was sitting in a pile of canary yellow, turquoise, and green sandals, navy and black pumps, and all kinds of hiking boots and flats. I held up a pair of satiny beige sandals and examined them. I guessed that they cost more than I made in a year at the department store.

I wondered again why the Seer lived out her old age in this house. Or did she? Did an unplanned event occur here, one in which she was swept away to a remote island or a castle? Surely it was a choice on her part to land in this quiet, dismal place of fog and close mouthed fishermen. Here, to be perceived as a witch, a Seer, or a misplaced poor person, an old fool at worst?

I slipped on one of the deep purple sandals. It fit perfectly, as though it was made for me. I stood up and slipped on the other sandal. I went to the bed and picked up the matching purple dress and held it up to the sunlight. I ran my eyes over the shape of the flowing, simple lines of it, smoothing my fingers over the thin, lightweight fabric, wondering about the places the Seer wore this dress.

Just as though it was the most natural thing in the world to do, I undressed down to my slip, then slid the purple dress over my head. The soft, thin folds whispered promises as it settled about my figure.

I looked in the oval mirror, turning this way and that, like a preening young girl. The dress fit perfectly. I looked carefree and sort of nice. I imagined my short hair swept up in curls framing my face, making it look mysterious and full of fine secrets. I imagined myself lounging gracefully at a ship's railing on a balmy evening full of stars, idly looking back at an island we were leaving.

I felt the deep, approving, soaking warmth of the sunlight pouring through the window while I tried on piece after piece of the Seer's extravagant clothing; every piece hinting and whispering of adventures in exotic, faraway places. And, they all fit.

÷

I organized the Seer's photographs into new albums and carried them downstairs and placed them on the bookshelves by the fireplace. I washed the Seers utility clothes and stacked them in a cupboard in the wash room so I could wear them for outside work.

I hand washed a few of the fine pieces and took the rest to the dry cleaners. I got her suitcases professionally restored and placed her shoes in fine, new boxes.

I found myself getting in the habit of working hard inside and out, cleaning myself up, then going upstairs and putting on the Seer's clothes for a little while before I changed and went home to Jim.

Then the time came when all was in place,

and I knew it. Something was finished. Something new was to begin, and I was the one who'd prepared the way for whatever it was. That afternoon, I went upstairs, changed into the purple dress and sandals, and wore them home to Jim.

I went shopping and bought a colorful sundress for me and a Panama hat for Jim. He looked at me oddly for a minute when I waltzed into the living room at home, holding a Panama hat in my hand. But I stayed steady and handed it to him with a flourish. He put it on, then waltzed me around the room.

Still, I could not bring myself to share the Seer's house with him. Not yet.

Spring turned to summer again, and I kept changing. I felt a confident newness growing steadily in me. I walked straighter and was gradually overcoming some of my terrible shyness. I started looking in the shop people's eyes when I bought teas.

The weather turned hot. I went to work on the outside of the house again. I painted the front porch pale blue and the railing around it grass green, and weeded the front yard. I replanted her garden at the back of the house. I filled it with earthy vegetables, nothing fancy. Potatoes and green runner beans and a few strawberry plants mounded up in a bright, sunny corner. Then I got down on my knees and checked the roots of the Victorian beige roses lining the rickety white picket fence. I pulled the dead flowers up and ordered new ones from her seed catalogues to replace them.

The house was beginning to look like it did

when I was a young and coltish girl walking past the Seers place every day. The only thing I didn't touch was the faded sign hanging by the front door.

At home, Jim finished his boat and made plans to take it for a trial run with his retired friends from work. I was tired and satisfied and happy every night, but I still didn't know what I was doing it for.

Jim tried to get me to rent out the Seer's house, but I wouldn't do it. Then he offered to move up the street with me when he saw how pretty I made it. I knew Jim wanted to get to know me the way I was when I was in the house up the street, but I couldn't share it with him. Not just yet. Just the colorful clothes I wore home sometimes, and the exotic meals, and a few books on history I thought he might like to read.

I kept on going and doing for both houses for the next few years until Jim suddenly passed away. It was his heart. It gave out on him. I grieved and then I sold my mother's house where Jim and I lived so many years, and moved into the Seer's house. I miss Jim, but I have to say it was good to not be in my mother's house any more.

The Seer's house is free and clear and just the way I want it to be. I have a pension from Jim and the money from mother's house to live on. These days I sit in front of the Seer's fireplace and read the books on the shelves and look through her albums when I look through mine. No one ever came here to ask about her. She is gone and forgotten, but not by me. Just like my kids and Jim won't be forgotten.

I believe the Seer told many good fortunes that helped others on their way. It is a rich and full thought that weaves my habitual silence into patterns of roads never traveled.

The travel books talk about places I will never see. They talk about people all over the world and all the exciting things they have done.

When I came across her books on reincarnation, I tell you, I was set free! I hope I come back next time a little bit bigger and a little bit braver. And I hope the Seer is in my life again. If she is, I will be bold and not afraid, and I will hand her that shiny dime once more and ask her to tell my fortune.

I sip tea from her fine old cups, talk to myself and the Seer and Jim and the kids, and yes, sometimes even my mother. I eat a little bit of what I want, when I want it, and I make things from the strange old recipes the Seer wrote in her fine hand. Through her journals and books, I understand people better.

I am daily re-discovering the old words that were already written into my soul from the beginning of myself. They are the same joyous words the Seer wrote in paint on the side of her cottage when I was a child. I remember them, and grow stronger. I accept the help of the Seers cottage. I never learned most of the Seer's secrets, never thought I could. But sometimes a little mystery in life is just the ticket.

÷

Which brings me to the fourth journal. It was hidden in the Seers bedroom in a deep pocket taped to the back of her mirror. It is filled with different kinds of love stories. Many names, addresses, letters, and notes are in it.

Each person I read about in it was connected to people who owned souls with words written on them like mine. Souls who would find meaning in the language the Seer once wrote on the walls of her cottage in paint. I began to wonder how many of those people were still alive.

The invitations to visit the Seer's cottage in July to help paint it went out to every one of her loves in the fourth album. Children, women, men. Many of them have passed away, I know, but maybe their ghosts will show up. Her home will be waiting, clean and fresh, the classic beige roses blooming, fresh paint ready and waiting to be applied to the walls of the Seer's cottage.

I am keeping my own journals now. I am leaving the Seer's cottage jointly to my children. Maybe they will open the front door on a fine summer day like I once did, and walk in and find the magic I found here. I'm planting a little magic of my own for them to find, with help from the Seer.

I will leave the journals and the Seers cottage as a doorway for my future generations to become more in life than just dutiful, good people. I was one of those, once upon a time, a time when I didn't know I could be all those things and more, by dreaming like a Seer.

You know, I never left this neighborhood. My brown hair turned white and I gained a bit of weight with each one of the children and kept it on. I gained a little more when Jim passed, leaving a big empty place in me I filled with food for awhile until I could tolerate the emptiness of it.

The closest I ever got to a vacation was going to the ocean two hundred miles away once with Jim so we could go fishing, which I hate, but went anyways because he wanted me to. That was a long time ago, and I know a dime has gone from a dollar to five since then. But I finally took the Seer's sign down from outside the front door, repainted it, and hung it back up. It still says, "I am a Seer and I will tell your fortune for a dime."

 Andy's Bus Ride Home

Andy was a driven man in more ways than one. To compensate, he worked as a cab driver in Seattle, where he drove with abrupt, unexpected lunges over its hills and whipped around the city's million curves and stop signs. He topped the speed limits over high bridges and careened through its numerous, dank, mysterious black tunnels and screeched around the unexpected sharp corners tucked everywhere.

His perilous driving threw the usual sedate passenger, forever damp and brooding like the Seattle weather, with their habit of enjoying complex lattes while thinking laborious, insular thoughts, lurching forwards and backwards and side to side in the back of his cab, making him feel very powerful. Their learned exhortations and exclamations therapeutically describing his unexpectedly bad behavior was wasted on him.

When Andy finally delivered his fares to their destination, he demanded exorbitant tips from them before they fled his cab. If they protested, so much the better, because he loved to argue and fighting was a thing he was familiar with.

Andy lived in a small room in a seedy men's hotel where the night life was chaotic and dangerous and the days were silent and deadly dull. Andy was small and wiry with long, wild black hair sticking out around his head like an unpruned shrub. He had the pale green eyes of a northern wolf lurking under bushy black brows and a nose flaring defiantly out over a small, tight mouth and a long chin; his hands were much too big. His was the permanent, ornery disposition of a mountain man who goes to bed hungry and rises too early.

From time to time, Andy picked up girlfriends from the streets outside the hotel and took them back to his room to stay with him. The proprietor didn't dare protest to him about the fact that it was a men's hotel he ran, and no women were allowed in it.

The girlfriends cooked and cleaned for Andy while he ordered them around and showed them his manly virtues. But before long, each one left to go back to the streets again, unchanged in any way by staying with him.

Andy's father, mother, and two sisters avoided him like the plague. They lived on the outskirts of the city in an upwardly mobile three story home, studiously avoiding any place they might encounter him.

Andy's mother and father were professionals, one a professor, the other a teacher. His siblings bowed to the inevitable. They attended college and became professionals too. Not Andy. Andy was a thorn in their side, a dark pestilence that never gave them a minutes peace until he disappeared at the tender age of eighteen into the heart of the city and out of their lives. They breathed a collective sigh of relief, and kept tabs on him from a distance. There would be no redemption for him, no coming after him, and he knew it.

The pain of his life caused Andy to take up

drinking and then quit. He wasn't going to let anything control him. He did drugs from time to time in an effort to unravel his knotty soul and stop the pain, but nothing worked, and no one offered to help him.

The cab company he worked for kept him on as an employee even though complaints came in from time to time from angry, disheveled passengers. They kept him because Andy knew every crack and crevice in the complicated city like the back of his hand. He knew all the odd little streets, all the freeways, and all the tourist sites in the city.

The cab company was chronically short of drivers, so they chose every day to overlook Andy's rough behavior. After all, no one was ever actually hurt while riding in Andy's cab, though they might have been shouted at.

÷

One day a couple hailed Andy's cab and asked him to give them a ride to their home. Andy drove like a madman. He screeched into the yard in front of their house on a hillside and jerked the cab to a stop, scattering gravel from the carefully tended driveway everywhere. Then he turned around and shouted at them to get out. They sat there, smiling and complimenting him on the great ride he'd given them.

"Far out!" they said to him. "What a thrill!" the couple said.

Andy was disgusted. He wanted them to be angry and quarrel with him. But they just sat there. "What a trip!" they grinned at each other and laughed in unison. Andy glared at them. Now he recognized them. They were "New Agers." Their type was all over the city. These two were most likely part of the crowd that drummed on mountain tops in the middle of the night, or held mysterious ceremonies in the city parks. Their kind ran around with tarot readers and goofy channelers, and were into tofu and other weird stuff.

"Get out!" he shouted again, and demanded a tip from them. They gave him a generous tip, gladly and willingly and waved goodbye to him as he spun out of their driveway.

A few days later, the couple called the cab company to compliment them on their cab driver, Andy. The company was very surprised.

Thus began a tradition. Whenever the couple needed to be driven anywhere, they called the cab company and asked for Andy. They didn't want anyone else to drive them.

Over time, from the back seat of the cab, while they bounced around like marbles, they introduced themselves and told him how much they appreciated his unique, vinegary, knotty ways. Andy snarled back at them from the front seat. They invited him to stop by any time and left their phone number and a twist of sage in the back seat for him. Andy took both items home and kept them.

The years flew by. Andy grew more lost and gnarled and wild. He drove his cab during the day and began walking the streets at night, ignoring the broken glass and the fights going on around him.

His heart shouted angrily through the dirty

city streets, searching everywhere, but everyone turned their faces from him in the black nights. Andy was looking for something to soothe his soul, something he could accept, but he couldn't find it. He was heading towards thirty, and nothing had changed him, and he was very irritated by that.

Each night in his room, he began burning a bit of the sage the "New Agers" left for him in the back seat of his cab. He burned it while he thought about life and the dirty deal it had handed him. He didn't know where he was in it. He lived hopeless and mad, and he suspected he might have to stay that way, and that just made his temperament worse.

The sage's pungent, acrid smell soothed him. He didn't try to find out why. The sage and its smell became a companion matching his personality, keeping his thoughts company whenever he burned it.

When the sage was used up, he hunted up the scrap of paper with the "New Agers" phone number on it. He called the couple up and demanded more sage. They said they were glad to hear from him and invited him to their home to pick up more sage.

Andy hated to be beholden to anyone. He had a huge headache from his anger by the time he reached their house. He swerved into the driveway, blew a few blasts on the horn and waited for them to come out. He kept the engine running. He planned to grab the sage out of their hands and drive away. But they came out empty handed and insisted he come in the house for a few minutes.

Silently he followed them into the house, his anger seething. They insisted he sit down on a sofa and have a cup of tea with them. The tea was hot and smooth and green, and there was milk in it. They served the tea to him in a big porcelain mug that was easy for him to wrap his too big, bony hands around. Then the couple put on a recording of soft, ancient chimes of music from an old cathedral album and sat across from him without speaking. Andy's headache started going away. He demanded several more mugs of the hot, soothing tea before he left with a fresh bundle of sage.

Andy began to turn to the couple more and more. At least twice a month he had tea with them and listened while they talked about where they'd been lately. They traveled all over the world to sacred places and prayed for all the souls of the people on Earth in each one.

The couple talked in a circle about young souls and old souls, until Andy came to understand that from what they were saying, he was an old soul, though he was young in his physical body. All of his life, his ways were those of a crotchety old mountain man. It was his destiny, his Karma, and he began to accept it.

Andy's gnarled and knotty ways smoothed out bit by bit as he began to search inside himself for the wisdom he knew he must carry from being an old soul. It had to be in there somewhere. The couple loaned him books to read, and he learned about the different kinds of wise men he was like.

He read about the old men who panned for gold in the high, rugged mountains surrounding

Seattle, and the old Ones who sat on those mountaintops while people came to them for wisdom. He began traveling to the mountains surrounding the city, seeing them with fresh eyes. But he still kept on having headaches. They grew more frequent and worse. Finally the doctors told him he had a brain tumor, and they didn't know how much longer he would live.

Andy quit his job at the cab company and moved in with a woman he met in a healing circle the couple took him to. He kicked her out of her house, then in a few weeks, he was forced to go to an adult care home to live.

Before long, Andy called the couple and asked them if he could spend the upcoming weekend with them. They said yes, and a yellow bus that drove disabled people around the city dropped him off at their house on Friday night.

The weekend was hard on all of them. Several times Andy ordered them to take him back to the home. He tried to kick them out of their house, and he shouted at them.

When the weekend was over, Andy got back on the yellow bus to go back to the adult care home. The couple breathed a sigh of relief. They said a prayer for him, and wished him well.

A month later, Andy suddenly passed away. He left word for his family to call the couple and tell them when the funeral service would be. During the service, wind blew the doors open, the flowers on his casket fell on the floor and the scent of sage permeated the air. Andy hated flowers.

After he was laid to rest, his father and mother and sisters constantly dreamed of him.

The air in their bedrooms filled with the smell of burning sage. In desperation, they moved away from the city to escape the bad dreams of Andy and the smell of sage.

The "New Age" couple that befriended him began having vivid dreams of Andy, too. In the dreams, he was angry and shouting at them. The smell of burning sage constantly floated through their house. One day a box of firecrackers that was stored away exploded for no reason. They knew it was Andy's anger exploding in the only way he thought he could, to get their attention.

Their patience with the pranks his ornery old soul kept playing on them was wearing thin. They began to pray and ask his gnarly, lost soul to get on with its journey instead of staying on Earth and pestering them. But nothing helped. Andy still hung around.

A few days later, the couple was sitting on their front porch basking in rare Seattle sunshine when a yellow bus turned into the driveway. On the side of the bus, printed in large black letters, were the words, "City Bus for the Disabled." The driver stopped the bus, got out and strode towards them. She said her name was Angela, and she was there to pick up Andy. The couple stared at her while a memory nudged their minds. They looked at each other at the same time and smiled.

Angela was tall, big boned, and spare. She was a giant of a woman. She had a wide smile and large white teeth. Her skin was tan and her huge mass of curly black hair, knotted and gnarled with silver, stood out several feet in a cloud around her shoulders and head.

Andy had once described a woman just like this to them as being his dream of what an angel should look like. He never told them she actually existed.

The couple told Angela that Andy passed away a few months ago. She said she was sorry to hear that. Then she said that someone put an order in for the bus to pick up Andy here today. Whoever called stressed that it was very important.

Then the beautiful woman said she'd driven Andy around quite a few times before. She said she'd known him for longer than they could imagine. The three of them reminisced about Andy's ornery ways for a few minutes, then Angela got back on the empty bus, closed the doors, and left.

The smell of sage left the house that same day. There were no more dreams of Andy. Later, the couple called the city to talk to Angela. There was something different about her they couldn't forget. They wanted to thank her for the completion she was a part of that day.

The city told them they didn't have a driver named Angela driving any of their vans.

"Vans?" the couple chorused. "Yes, we haven't used a bus in years," the person at the other end of the line stated firmly. "And, we are looking on our map as we are speaking with you, and we don't have a service van that serves your neighborhood, and never did."

The new age couple were mystified. They went down to the city's facilities to see if what they were told on the phone was true. It was.

They went home and that night, they lit
candles for Andy's old soul, and thanked him for
completing his earthbound journey by taking the
bus out of town with his Angel Angela.

10.   Sheila and the Silent Years

Each time my children leave
I turn childish as can be
when they drop in to visit
I become an adult again
controlled, calm and orderly.
I never let them see
that childish part of me.

My name is Tassy. Tassy Overton Bingham. I
married Mr. Charles Hartford Bingham a long
time ago and raised him and a bunch of brats.
That's the short version. He's gone. And those
brats are coming to visit again, and I'm going to
be ready for them, to pay them back for all the
times they've dropped in on me unexpectedly,
trying to find something they can use to put me
away somewhere.

That's what happened to Sheila. I learned my
lesson from what happened to her. Sheila used
to live across the street from me. Now she's
stuck in a home somewhere or dead, and her
house is being sold off by her brats. I plan to be
prepared. Sheila wasn't, and that was her
downfall.

When I found out the kids were coming, I
called in Ella to help me clean the house from
top to bottom and to hide my tools of creativity.
I'll hide my shawls and sheet music and the
boxes of chocolate covered cherries and the

candles I use when I do mantras, and the fake flowers I keep because I might not have enough time left to watch real ones bloom again. One never knows, so why take chances? I'll hide my stuff in closets, the attic, any place those snoopers might not look. I locked my hope chest and hid the key in my bra. I hope they don't stay long. If they do, I might forget where I put everything, that key included.

Veronica Lake and Paul Newman and cousins of mine who live in faraway places, Picasso and Steinbeck. Their names are painted on the brick floor of my screened in back porch. I hide the paint brushes I use to paint their names on each brick behind the roll of plastic on the back shelf of the pantry. The kids bought the plastic for me to cover the window seat cushions in the living room, but I like to run my hands over the nubbly fabric.

Ella and I wrestled the roll of green outdoor carpeting out of its place and spread it over the painted bricks on the back patio. We'll roll it back up after the kids leave.

Ella cussed and I laughed when she first helped me cut it down to the right size. That thin green carpet gets laid down over the patio floor whenever I want to hide the memorial growing beneath it from prying eyes.

Ella says I am being paranoid. She also says the paints I use on the bricks are too damn bright, but she agrees not to tell anyone on me.

"It's your own damn business." she says. Ella says "damn!" a lot, but that's because she has bunions, so I overlook it.

I painted Sheila's name on a brick. I used purple and bright yellow and painted little flowers along the edge of the brick to honor her gardening skills.

I suspect Sheila's kids sent her to a home to die in a faraway place so none of her friends could spring her from it. The ladies club we all belong to will go visit her as soon as we can find out where she is. We'll get the lay of the land, then we'll make a plan to spring her. We're thinking about hiring a detective to find her. It's all in the works.

Before those brats stashed her away somewhere, Sheila lived peacefully alone in her house across the street from me. God only knows who'll move in there now.

Sheila and me have been friends since we moved here and got initiated into the drill of pleasing demanding husbands and willful, spoilt children. Money doesn't always work the way you think it does.

We both joined the local women's club—women who led the same kind of lives we did. One by one, we lost our prosperous, pompous husbands, and one by one, we are having to learn to protect ourselves from our kids. Protection is what the green rug hiding the patio floor is all about.

Sheila's husband was one of those men who used up all the air in every room with his inflated, rigid opinions. That takes a toll on rooms too, you know. And houses and cars and people.

Us club ladies still get together and have lunch and play cards and do this and that. And

no, I'm not going to tell you what "this and that"
is...

Sheila's Story

Every afternoon, sunlight streamed through
the windows of her large, spacious bedroom just
at the top of the stairs. Sheila lay small and
thin, nestled in the big empty bed she'd slept in
for over fifty years. She lay quiet on large, soft
pillows, her fingers stroking the smooth texture
of the pillow cases she'd embroidered as a young
housewife.

Encased in the sweet, deep well of silence
filling the big empty house, she absently
watched the sunlight playing over the dresser
standing near the windows. The dresser was
large and lovely and of the finest quality. It was
part of the bedroom set gifted to her when she
turned eighteen. The lovely, large, golden brown
pieces were a high school graduation gift from
her parents. The message was clear; we're giving
you furniture because you're going to be married
to your husband's house...we expect you to be a
housewife, not a nuclear physicist or doctor or
God forbid, single.

In a sense, the bedroom set was her dowry,
for she slept in the bed with her husband from
the beginning of their marriage through the end
of it with his passing away. Their children were
born in the big bed. That was poetic; each of
them was conceived there too.

The dresser stood tall and wide, matching the

bed, it's rich brown whorls of fine wood covered with a satiny veneer. The set was an antique, the only one of its kind. The children valued it greatly. Sometimes, when they thought she was taking a nap or out of hearing range, she heard them arguing over the value of it and who would get it someday.

÷

The children, parents of a second generation of willful, self-righteous brats, had just left from their latest quick visit. They'd stopped by on their way to the beach where they planned to spend the summer. Sheila looked at the pictures of their beach house. A tumbled pile of cubes with glass sides. Just looking at it made her shins and elbows hurt; the edges looked deadly sharp.

Sheila sighed with relief when they left. She took the medication the doctor prescribed that only she and the doctor knew about. She took it every afternoon, then lay on her bed listening to the ticking clock until she lapsed into the nap the doctor insisted she take.

Sheila took her medicine and lay in her bed, waiting to fall sleep. Over time, she became familiar with the patterns the sunlight made on the walls and the golden path it made across the hardwood floor. She noticed how tall the white painted baseboards were, and how deep the window sills were.

After awhile, she became eager for the enforced afternoon nap that kept her health stable. As soon as she lay down, she began examining the bedroom that now held only her and no demanding husband or children.

She measured the sunlight streaming through the large windows, keeping the time of its comings and goings in her mind. After awhile, she knew exactly when it came, how strong it stayed, and when it left.

She thought about the heat and light the sunlight provided. The sun moved through the bedroom windows all year long even though autumn flew by so fast and the winter months were long.

÷

She thought about how her husband and children never liked plants and flowers, but she needed and loved them. She'd given them up because all the space in the house was needed to contain her husband and children's wants and needs. She'd planted a few small plants in a corner of the back yard, but they complained about that too. She'd limited her love for gardening until the children were grown and her husband passed away.

She thought about the necessary to life naps she took every day. My, they took up a lot of time! Wouldn't it be lovely to have something natural and innocent and beautiful growing in her room, something she could watch growing while she waited for sleep? Heck, she might pass away in her sleep. Maybe the last thing she ever saw in this world would be a flower blooming.

She made up her mind. Seeds. She would plant them. No one was here to stop her now. She would wake up to living, pretty flowers being the first thing she saw when she opened her eyes. She'd feel the same rush of joy she'd felt for her husband when they were newly married, and for her children when they were first born. She'd yearned almost too long to feel that way about something again.

÷

She looked around her bedroom. The solid, well made bedroom set belonged just to her. In a house where everything belonged to everyone else, it was hers alone. The set reminded her of her mother and father. She thought about them, and knew they'd understand what she planned to do, wherever they were. She also accepted that with her heart problem, she wouldn't have the energy to do it all at once. She would have to take her time, do it in stages.

Each day she did what she could. Before she climbed onto her big, empty bed to take a nap, she removed a few things from the dresser drawers and stacked them neatly in the empty cardboard boxes she'd brought down from the attic and placed by her bed.

She worked at it each day until one day, the dresser drawers were empty, and the cardboard boxes were full. It took days and effort to pull the empty drawers out of the dresser and stack them beside it, but she managed.

She pulled and tugged at the empty dresser frame, moving it a few inches across the room each day until it stood just where she wanted it. It took a couple of days to get the dresser angled just right to catch the sun's rays   pouring

125

through the windows. She stood back and admired the dresser's satiny, polished wood. How rich and beautiful it glowed in the sunlight when she put the drawers back in!

Sheila lay on her bed contemplating the dresser and calculating angles at naptime. She pulled each drawer out to different lengths and watched where the sun's rays hit them. She ended up with the second drawer pulled out to the desired distance. She closed the other drawers.

It took more days to carry half buckets of the rich, dark soil stored in the potting shed up to her bedroom. She poured it into the second dresser drawer until it was a fraction past half full. She smoothed the rich dirt out with her hands, savoring the texture and smell of it. She banked and angled the dirt to get the full benefit of the summer sun. Then she opened the flower seed packets she'd ordered from a nursery and sprinkled them in the open dresser drawer. She watered them, covered them with a layer of soil, and waited for them to grow.

$$\div$$

She napped fitfully each day, watching the little flower shoots pop up through the rich, dark, sweet smelling dirt in the drawer. She remembered her children when they were babies. She remembered how young her husband looked laying in his casket on the day he was buried.

Memories of a lifetime flowed through her thoughts during each nap, matching the rhythm and steady growth of the flowers. She changed her thinking about things along with their growth, creating fertilizer and making useful, cleansing soap out of the most painful of her memories.

Memory keeping wasn't simple any more. She was becoming emotionally liberated by connecting realizations. Her soul was freed from an old prison, enthralled and interested in life again. Nap time became a sacred ritual, a time for deep re-thinking of old memories and consequent prayers asking angels, guides and beings to help her and her family. She was filled with gratitude for the solitude and the great gifts of flowers, scents, and memories.

Filled with awe, she garnered realizations about larger aspects of Life. She wove patterns of knowledge as to how she and her generations fit into Life, and how her children and their generations could fit into life happily again. Hope for changes in her children grew steadily along with the seeds planted in the dresser drawer.

÷

The doctor's prescriptions grew stronger. Sheila grew thinner, but her joy never wavered. She called in painters to paint her bedroom orange to enhance the light pouring into her room each afternoon.

One day she decided she wasn't willing to have the flowers grow for just one season. She made plans to plant winter flowers in the dresser drawer when the summer flowers finished blooming, maybe calendulas, begonias, a

Christmas cactus.

÷

The mingled scents of the flowers blooming in the dresser drawer hung sweet in the air in her bedroom the afternoon the children dropped by unexpectedly. They planned to spend the night on their long drive home from their summer vacation. They'd left their summer place early. They'd endured enough of the quiet of it, and of listening to their children whining about missing their friends.

Sheila didn't know they were coming. They never called, as usual. They took it for granted she would be there and welcome them. She was old; they felt they had a right to appear at any time without apology, to intrude on her privacy at will, and to judge her living habits safe or unsafe. They believed their judgments gave them the right, they called it their duty, to make decisions for her as though she were a child.

Sheila was napping when they let themselves into her house with their house key. Their voices woke her from pleasant dreams. She was startled and couldn't speak when they stomped into her bedroom.

They ran their eyes over the room. They saw the orange walls and boxes of her clothes on the floor next to the bed. They saw the dresser sitting at a crazy angle with a mass of flowers blooming in an open drawer. They saw the gardening gloves and the watering can sitting on the window sill.

Sheila sat up and put her feet over the side of

128

the bed. Hope welled up in her. She grew excited and started to speak, to tell them her ideas for the coming winter. She planned to gather materials to make scrapbooks she could paint and draw in and place old photographs in. She wanted them to know her life story, her feelings and the history of their family, both its strengths and weaknesses.

She'd given much thought to their meanness and the emptiness it sprung from during her naps, and she yearned to change their legacy. She felt she knew how to do that at last! She wanted to share her essence with them and the wisdom she'd gleaned from the cycles of life that had turned and spun for her this summer, making her into who she was now.

÷

But before she could say anything, they grabbed the dresser and dragged it roughly across the golden plank floor. She watched them shove it back where it stood all the years they were growing up. One of them pounded down the stairs and rushed back with a bucket. They jerked the flowers out of the drawer, tossed them in the bucket, and hurried them away. They scooped the dirt out of the drawer and into a wastebasket. They cleaned and vacuumed out the drawer, scolding her all the while.

Sheila sat on the side of the bed, watching, listening to their scolding voices and mean words. They worked busily around her, shouting at each other, making a din of noise.

Sheila's heart pounded painfully. They were

methodically destroying the blossoming core of who she was, and who they might have become had they let her be.

She retreated to a lonely place inside herself, a place filled with a blizzard of white, cold snow. She looked out the window in surprise. The sun was gone and it was snowing. When did that happen? She thought it was sunny and quiet when she fell asleep a little while ago. Well, she must have dreamed it.

Sheila never saw the need to speak to her children again. They assumed she'd suffered a stroke that rendered her speechless, and hastily summoned help. Sheila was rushed to the hospital. In a few weeks, her children moved her to a nursing home close to them, far from her home.

They sold her house. The oldest daughter claimed her bedroom set and had it stripped and painted to match her own décor.

÷

They visited her once in awhile, at Easter or Christmas, and chattered at her like birds that are never quiet. They kept their visits sanitary, supervised, and short. They fumbled with the three faded plastic flowers stuck in the tiny vase she was allowed to keep on the night stand by her bed. She knew they wanted to toss the plastic flowers in the wastebasket, but they knew the staff would take them to task for it. They knew the fake flowers had somehow been put there because of what they had done to her.

Sheila always turned her head away and

130

stared out the window as soon as she heard them rehearsing what they'd say to her as they came closer and closer.

It was a fluke of seasons and of her life, but it was always snowing. The weatherman was predicting another blizzard. Sheila shivered. She told herself it was time to batten down the hatches. Winter had set in. This was no time to grow flowers. No, not yet. Silence surrounded her, deep and knowing, keeping its own counsel.

The last time the children visited, a large fresh orange lay glowing with life on her tiny bedside table. The plastic flowers were gone. The orange's bright, hopeful fragrance filled the air. It was the only color in the room.

11.   The Alamoosa Fish Supper

"Do yew' lak' ta' feesh?"

Jessup threw the question at her in a loud voice just as she scurried past the card table he sat at. She skidded to a stop and glared at him. His timing was perfect, she thought bitterly. He sat there grinning at her innocently. He was playing dominoes with three friends so she hoped it wasn't her he addressed his question to. She weighed the odds and lost, stopped and slowly turned around.

The senior center was busy as usual, filled to the brim with old white or purple haired people playing cards, old bald men playing pool, heavy or bony oldies playing dominoes with each other, all eating snacks, soft things like tapioca pudding, cottage cheese or white bread sandwiches. Things that didn't require too many teeth, or too much physical labor.

Dolly Vorton, the gray haired senior who ran the center for the town, paused by her desk at the sound of Jessup's loud voice. Her eye glassed glare fixed on the female who turned to look at him. Evidently, she was to blame for Jessup's folly. Dolly was a stickler for keeping the noise down.

"Yes, I do," she answered cautiously, avoiding the word 'feesh.'

"Well, why don't I jist' pick you up in the mornin' and wee'll go feeshen, then?" Jessup's loud, suggestive voice rang through the senior center again. Though she didn't see them, she heard everyone stop what they were doing. She felt their squinty, wrinkled eyes fasten on her. Suddenly old age "love" was aloft, trumpeted into the stale air of the senior center by Jessup's loud, leering voice.

"What a troubling thing energy is," she thought. The attention instantly fastened itself on her like lost crusts on bread, thanks to big mouth Jessup. She felt the energy of the old peoples anger, their constipated fear and desperation surging towards her as if looking for a less-old life to cling to and suck dry.

Some of them hesitated. They were the more evolved ones; they acknowledged a surly acceptance of their condition. Most people didn't have a clue about energy manners. They couldn't tune into the energies on the unseen planes of existence and correct their bad manners, so they stayed rude and took, took, took.

The worst were the secret hopes many of them held onto. The hope of a late life romance to cure their aging, a second chance to banish an illness, but mostly the hope that their children would give a damn whether they lived or died, which wasn't going to happen.

She looked around. Loneliness and secret hopes that could never come true filled this room, this place she was suddenly trapped in. She felt the weight of the negative energy the aged crowd exuded, and it began to press her down into the floor.

The little town held polite classes on "Aging and its Problems" once a month. She attended one class. That was enough. There were intermittent waves of hollow laughter from crude jokes about scenarios of their impending demises. The evening ended with a half-hearted invitation from the moderator to enjoy the "snacks" provided by the volunteers. Always, the food. She shrugged. What else was there?

She wasn't in that universe yet. She was still just a bit too young, though dancing close to the edge of it. A toehold only. The only reason she went to the senior center was to use the exercise equipment. No one else used it. She didn't like playing cards and sitting around chatting with seniors of which many seemed addicted to denture cream. The oldies were regular attendees; at least as much as their probiotics permitted. She figured some of them showed up and stayed a bit until they remembered where they were supposed to be.

÷

Lost in bitter thought, she swayed back and forth until the old people's smells invaded her aura. That eager activity galvanized her into action. She needed to get this over with, try to be polite and get the hell out. Away from the combined, creeping aromas emitted from the female dominated, haphazard and habitual collection of aged bodies around her.

Once upon a time, she'd taught metaphysics. She knew that on the unseen energy planes, many groups of people collectively and eagerly dumped their negative energies from every level of their being on whoever was near. The younger the better, though some of the oldies in this

134

place were consciously aware enough to leave the smaller children alone.

The people who were dumped on went away repulsed, carrying away the smells and unwelcome energy burdens of the dumpers to process for them, not knowing what just happened. Some got sick or depressed from it, and their unconscious protected them by never allowing them to return for a second round. A few others kept coming back for more, out of guilt or whatever, gaining weight or losing mental faculties. Some groups did this, others didn't. As far as she was concerned, this one did.

÷

"Okay..." she dragged the word out, thinking, correctly as it turned out, that people living in this part of the world left a lot unsaid.

"Yeahaah," he drawled. "We'll meetcha' at Ma's Café at six o'clock for bacon and biscuits."

Jessup spoke about breakfast foods with authority and panache. He pulled up his dangling left suspender and parked it on his hefty shoulder.

"...then we'll ride out to Lake MacMurky and drop in a line for two or three hours."

She thought about it while everybody who wasn't on oxygen held their breath and waited.

She shook her head. "Nope. That ain't gonna' happen. I'm not eating bacon and biscuits at six in the morning for anybody."

The guys around the card table sat silent as deacons in high church pews, listening and shaking their heads in disapproval at her insanity. She jumped in with a question before anyone of them could object.

"Who all's a' goin?"

The guys at Jessup's table and those nearby moved in unison, like dry leaves settling on the ground after a short, gusty wind tossed them around. Her question forced him to spell it out, and he didn't like to just say.

"Well, Barton and George here."

He waved his arm at two men sitting at the table, then flung his other arm toward two geezers nearby and drawled, "Wade and Orville allus' meet us there."

Then his eyes brightened with unanticipated inspiration and he bellowed cheerfully for those who were hard of hearing, "Or we could go by ourselves, and let Barton and George here ride with Wade and Orville."

She studied Jessup a minute and said, "Yeah, well, that ain't gonna' happen!"

Jessup laughed and puffed out his chest, rolling his eyes around at the silent people watching them. "She's just playing hard to get." his eyes told them.

"Such a ham!" she thought.

George ignored Jessup, cleared his throat importantly and asked, "What's the matter, ye' cain't' eat a little breakfast before you go feeshin? You cain't expect to catch feesh' when you ain't' et' nothin'. A big breakfast's jist' the ticket! You'll stay a little sisee' if you cain't do no better than that!"

Barton added slowly and solemnly in his deep voice, "Yeah." He started to nod his head but disremembered why, forcing him to take almost a minute to get the word out.

÷

They picked her up at seven the next morning after a lengthy negotiation about the time their daily breakfast at Ma's might be finished. The front passenger side of Jessup's dusty, green four wheeler was empty. Jessup ogled her from his seat behind the steering wheel. Evidently, the empty front seat was for her.

George and Barton grumbled in soft waves at her from the backseat while she climbed in.

"You shore' are a lot a' trouble fer' us!"

They nodded their heads at each other in agreement, believing their half smiles at each other were hidden from her. With satisfaction, they predicted future disasters.

"And you probably always will be!"

They shook their heads at each other while she watched. She knew exactly what they were thinking.

It would have been much easier for them to buy her breakfast, but no, she wouldn't do it. She'd disrupted the smooth flow of their years of following the same routine. A routing breached by a woman who did weird things on the dusty, weird exercise contraptions in a corner room at the senior center. All because Jessup had taken a shine to her.

"What time did you get up this morning?" Barton asked smoothly. All three guys smirked at her. She wasn't about to tell them she was usually up by five or six in the morning. She turned and stared at the two old men in the back seat, taking in their various conditions before she answered. George was tapping his chest to make sure his pace maker was still working, and Barton was counting blood pressure pills to make sure he took one earlier. She glanced at Jessup. He was picking his teeth with a wood tooth pick. She turned back around and pretended to cover a huge, noisy yawn.

She listened as the two old men behind her gave soft, martyred sighs. One said, "Yep, just what we figured!" The other said something that sounded like, "...just like a wombat," which she assumed was "woman." They talked about her as if she wasn't there while Jessup meandered at a snail's pace down dusty back roads towards Lake MacMurky. She pretended she didn't hear George mutter as he tried to explain her to himself and anyone else listening.

"She's never been to any of the lakes around here. She's been too busy working. Just like a Yankee."

The other chorused, "Yup!"

They drifted down the dusty roads between slices of silence and soft mutterings. The sweet, cool morning air hummed softly around them.

"Ya' ever fished before? Now tell me true." Barton finally asked in a condescending tone.

"A few times." she answered casually, sticking her hand out the open window to let the cool breeze ripple over it.

"What'd ye fish fer'?"

She waited a minute, then said, "Oh, croppies, blue gill, don't like catfish." She felt the stir of interest behind her in the Bronco.

"Is that right? Well, WE all like catfish."

George insisted, Barton echoing him. She heard the joshing note of jubilation in their voices. Evidently, they didn't believe a word she said.

"Yeah," she spoke carelessly, as though it didn't matter. "I got so I was catchin' three pound croppies on four pound test."

She leaned back and stared straight ahead, listening in satisfaction as they sucked in their collective breaths. Silence fell. The questions stopped. She hoped she hadn't given them heart attacks. She didn't dare look back at them.

÷

Jessup drew up on a small bluff overlooking the lake. He put the Bronco in park and climbed out. He was portly and it took a minute's struggle. George and Barton sat perfectly still and waited. They didn't try to get out. Puzzled, she sat still and waited too, wondering what was supposed to happen next.

He walked to the back of the vehicle and opened it up. "You jist' goona' set there?" he roared at her. She jumped, startled, then drew in a deep breath. Instructions. At last. Good. She climbed out and walked to the back of the Bronco. He handed her two fishing poles. She waited while he helped George out and set his walker on go mode. George took another blood pressure pill and coughed. Barton unfolded himself slowly and carefully out of the Bronco with Jessup tugging on him.

"Good old Bronco, Good Old Bessie!"

Barton leaned on the faded green Bronco's fender to get his bearings and breath. Then he

139

helped George maneuver the walker down the short path to the walkway leading to the dock.

Jessup ignored their slow journey. He followed behind them patiently as if he were a snail carrying fishing rods, a tackle box and a pail. She followed him down the short path to the long, thin floating wood walkway leading out to the dock and fishing shanty. The walkway had metal railing to hold on to, and posts every few feet. She was relieved.

She glanced at the two men waiting by the fish shanty. They were white haired and wore blue coveralls over plaid shirts. They watched her follow Jessup down the dock. Jessup looked back at her and flashed a brilliant smile. When they reached them, Jessup said, "This here's Wade. This here's Orville. Orville likes to sing at the sing-alongs on Friday nights down at the senior center."

The man named Orville broke into a mournful Hank Williams song about not getting out of this world alive.

She stared at him in horror. How bad could this little fishing trip get? So far, it was getting worse by the minute. She fingered the cell phone in her pocket. Should she call 911 or her new friend Flossy to come and get her?

Orville stopped singing. The man named Wade thumped him on the back. Orville finally got his breath back. He broke out into a huge smile and looked at her for praise. She pasted a thin, watery smile on her face.

Jessup was watching her. She suspected he knew exactly what her true reaction was. He bellowed in a loud voice, startling her.

"She ain't et' nothin' this mornin', that's what's the matter with her."

He grinned cajolingly at her.

"Orville here sings anytime anybody will let him," he boasted on Orville's behalf. Orville broke into song again. She barely managed to keep from covering her ears and sprinting for shore.

"I forgot my purse." she muttered. It was true, and the one time she could honestly say she was thrilled about it. She turned and hurried away. When she looked back at the men, they were circled, their backs to her, chattering like magpies.

÷

She composed herself and moseyed back down the walkway, her purse slung over her shoulder. She stopped just as Jessup threw his hands out in a wide gesture that included Lake MacMurky and nearby parts of the state. His chubby pink face and big, sky blue eyes shone. She suspected he'd been bragging about her being with him. The guys looked everywhere but at her.

The two men gave grudging nods and mumbled hello again. She nodded back at them. Evidently they were starting over, but Orville didn't offer to sing. There was a God!

As one, the men turned their backs to her. George and Barton set up their fishing gear and eased down onto empty upside down five gallon white paint pails.

141

÷

Jessup propped their rods against the metal wall of the fish shanty and set his bright yellow bucket with the laundry soap label down. "Ain't this a purty place?" he asked, swinging his hands out in another expansive gesture that included clutching at her.

She evaded his busy, fanciful hands and nodded. He grinned and plucked a small towel and a jar of bait out of the bucket, worked on her fishing rod, and handed it to her. He waited for her approval. She looked it over. There was a respectable croppie lure, and tiny squares of stinky croppie bait on it.

"Nice."

He grinned and fixed his own bait and lure. She turned in a slow circle, rod in hand, taking in the green tree line, the blue sky and the gentle waves rocking the floating fish shanty.

She turned to him and said, "I like it!"

Jessup grinned. He stared at Wade and Orville's backs for a minute, then at George and Barton's backs.

"They're none used to a woman likin' fishin!" Jessup suddenly bellowed at their backs.

Their shoulders tightened, but none of them turned around. She jumped, startled at his odd tendency to bellow. She narrowed her eyes and glared at him. He returned her look with an innocent, wide eyed, baby blue stare. He grinned and waited.

Ah! She caught on. They must be hard of hearing.

"Well, they'll jist' hafta' git over it!" she

bellowed back, answering the challenge in his words in the accent she grew up with.

"Now, are we gonna' fish or not?"

÷

From time to time, responding to a secret, unseen signal, the men moved to a new fishing spot. She watched them and moved when they did.

In a few minutes, the fish started biting. She hooked a nice croppie. She hesitated as she pulled it up. What should she do? There were options. Each option would take her down a different path. This whole thing began as a one day lark; she wondered if it could become more.

The senior center was deadly dull at best. Lonely after she moved to the little town where she knew nobody, she went to the center to use the workout equipment in the hopes somebody else would be using it too. When Jessup invited her to go fishing, the whole room perked up with excitement.

She'd told the men that she'd fished years ago. She didn't tell them that she knew how to catch, clean, and fry fish six different ways to Sunday. Let alone baste, boil, poach and roast. In the past, all she had to do was take a fish off the line now and then and look adoringly into her husband's sky blue eyes. But he was gone now. Those days were gone.

÷

She glanced around. The old men were watching her, waiting to see what she did with the fish. Except for Jessup. He was fishing on the other side of the shanty. If she pulled the fish up and handled it like she knew what she was doing, like she'd watched her husband doing so many times, they would quickly lose interest. On the other hand, if...

She bellowed, "Jessup!" in as high a girly voice as she could manage. The old men watched in triumph as Jessup came pounding around the shanty and screeched to a stop in front of her.

"What's the matter?"

She bellowed again in a high, girly voice, "Kin' you take this fish off the line for me?"

"What?"

Dumbfounded, Jessup stared at her. "You screamed like you was a' dyin!" he roared accusingly as he took the fish off the hook. The old men listened and laughed silently, their shoulders shaking with the effort.

"Ya' laked' ta' give me a heart attack!"

He shouted happily, eyeballing the men.

The old men turned their backs to them again and began happily muttering to each other.

"Told ya' so!" one of them said. She lowered her eyes. "I won't scream so loud anymore." she bellowed.

"Better not!' He leered at her and ambled off. She caught more fish and bellowed for Jessup each time. He took the fish off the hook and rebaited it for her while bellowing complaints about "girly girls."

Finally, he gave up.

"I'll have to fish beside ye' so's I can help ye'." He bellowed this mournful news to the other fisherman and everyone within hearing distance in the county. She couldn't decide if he knew what she was up to or not, so she batted her eyes at him every now and then anyway, and he leered back at her to entertain the other old men.

÷

Barton and George caught a big croppie and brought it in together after a long struggle. They were proud of it, and insisted she have her picture taken with them and the fish.

"Sissy Girl, git' over here!" they hollered in unison in a loud, breathless, proud whisper. She blinked at their weird shout. It crossed her mind that their unified sound effect could easily mimic the eerie, ear-catching theme in a bad horror movie.

She minced over, shoved between them, grabbed the walker and hid it behind them. The old men leaned against her, swaying while she hugged them close to hold them steady for the picture. They smelled of old age, medicine, the outdoors, and goodness, just like her father smelled during the last years of his life. Orville and Wade took the picture. They stood close together, using an ancient Polaroid camera, instructing each other on how to do it. When the picture unfurled from the camera, Orville grabbed it and flapped it in the air like he was Ward Bond signaling a wagon train to circle up.

"Hold it still, Orv, hold it still." Wade insisted,

trying to grab the slick photograph.

The Polaroid was blurry. Orville and Wade said she moved her head and caused the blur. She bit her tongue; they were the blurry ones, with their tremors and jerky limbs!

The Polaroid cleared up. The old men in it stood handsome and proud with their fish held high. The picture would wind up on the bulletin board at the senior center until it disappeared under mysterious circumstances.

÷

Another hour passed. Wade's face was turning a dull, pasty gray. Orville sat motionless on his bucket, glassy eyed, pretending to fish. George was rubbing his chest and Barton was counting pills. She glanced at Jessup. He didn't seem to be bothered by anything so mundane as time, hunger, or heat. Every so often one of the old men eyed her and sighed loud enough to wake the dead. Their sighs stayed just short of a groan. They took turns.

She was puzzled. Why didn't they just pack up and leave? Was there some kind of silent contest going on? She suspected she was the cause of whatever it was.

She concentrated on the puzzle they were presenting to her and realized they were all willing to die out here before they'd throw in the towel and ask to go home before a female did! She sighed. Men! ...

A breeze stirred the water into choppy little white capped waves. She turned her gaze to the shore. The trees lacing the red and yellow ochre banks were dark green. Birds flew lazy and content through the air. She listened to the rhythm of the waves slapping against the dock, and felt the slight rocking motion when a boat slowly motored past. It was perfect. She could stay here all day.

"But..." she sighed and looked at the men. She looked around for Jessup. He was fishing at the other end of the dock.

"Jessup!" she bellowed in a high, whiny voice.

He jumped like he was shot and glared at her. She snickered behind her hand. He jerked his fishing rod out of the water and hurried over to her.

"What the hell's the matter now?" he bellowed.

She winced at his loud voice and glared at him. He was still putting on a show. He seemed to know exactly what she was thinking. He swayed closer and leered at her, making sure all the other old men were watching. She put the back of her hand to her brow, frowned up at him in an expression she hoped was called "simpering," then, for good measure, tapped her foot.

He stared at her, an astounded look on his face, a knowing twinkle in his eye. Evidently, they were in this together. Well, she always did had a flair for acting. Evidently, he did too.

She snuck a glance at the old men. They were frowning at her. She knew she would have to walk a fine line with this high wire act. She raised her voice until it was high and accusing, then shoved her hands in front of Jessup's face and wiggled her fingers.

"I just got this manicure two days ago, see? And it's getting hot out here or didn't you notice? And, you didn't warn me to bring a hat!"

Jessup looked confused and stayed silent, letting her play it out. In a petulant, scolding voice she asked, "Is there any extra water? Is it cold, so I can drink it? Do you have any sunscreen I can put on for this third degree sunburn I'm getting? And what about lunch? Do we have to stay much longer? In other words, don't you think it's time to go home, mister?"

He stared at her as though she was a dunderhead. She swept one hand out towards George, Barton, Orville, and Wade, who was now resting against a dock post, his eyes closed. Jessup's eyes followed her hand. "Oh." he said, comprehending the dilemma at last.

She nodded at him and smiled at him as though he was a three year old.

"Dummy!" she hissed under her breath.

Loudly she said, "You can fish until hell freezes over, but not everybody wants to! I wanna' go home right now!"

He rocked back on his heels and studied his fishing buddies. She rolled her eyes at him and waited for his verdict. She jumped when he unexpectedly bellowed. "Well, girly girl, are you ready to call it quits for the day? Are you ready to go home?" His eyes never left his pals; their eyes never lit on him but on every other thing, even a bobbing beer can in the water, though they listened to every word.

"And, girly girl, you need a cap, not a hat!"

Relief washed over her. She took the cue from him. It was true. She was supposed to ask to go home first. She shouted back.

"I've been ready to go home for the last hour! I don't intend to fry to a frazzle in this sun or mess up my manicure; besides, my fingers smell like fish!"

She wiggled imaginary long red nails at Jessup. He grabbed her hand and kissed it, courtly and quick as could be. She jumped back and glared at him while the old fishermen snickered. Jessup grinned at her with his large, innocent baby blues. She was extremely tempted to ask him how many women he'd caught with them, but wisely, kept her mouth shut.

She pretended she didn't see Jessup roll his eyes at the other men and wink before he said, "Gimme' yer' rod, and I'll put it away fer' ye!" He widened what he told her earlier were his "fetching big blue eyes" at her disarmingly while the rest of the gang watched.

Orville and Wade stowed their poles and bait in their buckets and slowly made their way down the walkway with George and Barton following. At the top of the short hill, they parted, Orville and Wade towards Wade's old black Chevy. Jessup stored the fishing gear and the fish they'd caught in the back of the Bronco. Then he helped George and Barton into the Bronco. None of them talked on the way home. George wheezed like a steam engine while Barton counted pills and muttered numbers in a shaky voice. Jessup ignored them and grinned at her from time to time.

They dropped her off first. When she got out, Jessup grinned at her and bellowed, "Do ye' thaink' ye' might wanna' go feeshin' agin? How 'bout tomarra' morning?"

She studied him soberly, then looked at the men in the back seat. George was holding his chest and nodding yes. Barton shook a shaky finger in her vicinity accusingly. "Bring a little girly girl cap ta' ware' ta'morry!" he warbled in broken notes.

She looked back at Jessup, who was grinning like there wasn't a care in his world, no worries, no sick old men with him, just fine healthy men and him and her. He held her look while she studied him. She tried to take his measure, but couldn't quite.

"I'll be ready," she finally said. She turned and walked away, grinning to herself.

"We'll be by a little earlier than today!" Jessup bellowed.

She nodded without looking back, hearing their laughter as Jessup spun out of the driveway.

She set her clock early, not knowing what to expect. They showed up in the dark at six. Styrofoam boxes were sitting on George and Barton's laps. They wore sour looks mixed with anticipation on their faces.

"Hurry up!" Jessup chided, as she pretended to stumble sleepily out of the house. She turned to lock the door. She fumbled with the key until Jessup started to get out. She locked her door quickly, pocketed the key and ambled slowly towards the waiting vehicle of old men.

Jessup bellowed, "Cain't ye' move a little faster? We' wanna' watch the sun come up over the lake! And we'd like ta' git there afore' dark sets in agin'!"

She yawned widely behind her hand and tried her best to look sleepy. "Okay!" she muttered, as if she didn't know quite where she was. A chorus of voices scolded her while she placed her large purse on the floorboard and climbed slowly into the passenger side.

"Okay! Okay!" she muttered at them.

"Put yer' seat belt on!" Jessup shouted.

She peered at him.

"Okay!" she shouted grouchily back at him.

He shut up and waited until she wrestled the seat belt on amid a chorus of impatient male voices.

Suddenly Jessup gunned the motor and they took off like a bat out of Hell, bouncing out of her driveway, throwing her back against the passenger seat. She waited for a word of complaint from the back seat passengers, but they wisely kept their mouths shut. Were they alive back there? Did they need to detour to the hospital so they could be treated for whiplash?

She glanced back at them. They stared back at her with carefully blank faces that said, "Who me? I don't know nothin'!"

As soon as she turned back around, she heard the stealthy rustling of Styrofoam boxes behind her. The smell of bacon and eggs wafted up to her.

Finally a voice spoke in the darkness. "Didn't have time ta' eat ye' breakfast this mornin', did ye, little girl?" George questioned in a rich, satisfied voice.

÷

She considered her answer. She'd already walked two miles and downed a breakfast of eggs, fruit, toast that would make a marathon runner envious.

"How come ya' got here so early?' she whined. Barton, George, and Jessup sucked in collective sighs of satisfaction. Jessup rustled around in the brown bag he'd stowed between their seats and handed her a huge white biscuit she knew must weigh at least three pounds.

"Here. This is from Ma's!" he spoke with a culinary experts pride. "I'll take ye' thare' sometime when yer' willin' ta' go to a decent place ta' eat."

She pried open the doughy biscuit and cautiously peered inside. On a field of undercooked white flour repined two skinny, undercooked slices of fatty bacon. She hefted the lard heavy biscuit in her hand and gave a great sigh.

"Thanks a lot!" she said in a voice of anguish laced with a tiny dose of cheer.

She picked at the biscuit edges and stared out the window while the men finished their breakfasts and took their medicines.

When they got to Lake MacMurky, she jumped out of the Bronco, grabbed her purse and minced down the hill to the walkway leading out to the fishing shanty. She stopped halfway down the walkway and waited.

Just as they reached her, she jerked a huge roll of snow white wipes out of her oversize purse and started wiping down the metal walkway railings. She ignored the old men shuffling past her, scolding her for "runnin' away on 'em." She listened until they settled themselves on the dock around the fish shanty. Steadily she moved down the walkway towards them, wiping the metal railing while she went. The silence rolled on and on. She kept rubbing and waited.

Finally George asked, "Whatcha' doin' that fer'?" The rest of them waited for her answer. She rolled her eyes at him. "So I can lean against the railing while I fish," she explained, as though the answer was obvious, and he must be joshing her.

Orville, Wade, George, Barton, and Orville's friend Joe gaped at her. Jessup turned his back to her. His shoulders started shaking. She glared at him. No help there. She was on her own. He wouldn't turn around. She suspected he was laughing too hard.

"I have to get rid of the spiders and cobwebs," she explained ruefully, waving a white wipe in the air like it was a truce flag.

"Oooh! Girly girl is afraid of a few little bugs?"

She nodded reluctantly. The guys went off and huddled and talked. She kept on wiping. The huddle broke up. Barton motioned at the guys who stood in a little cluster behind him. They all nodded their heads. She watched them, picturing an aged football team on its last leg. Yep. Men. Football. Uh huh.

"Maybe we oughta' all pitch in and buy ye' a little pair of pink rubber boots so ya' kin stomp them little bugs ta' death!" Barton announced.

They snickered and trembled with laughter. She frowned at them like she was taking their suggestion seriously.

"I do like pink," she conceded with a frown. She waved her hands defensively and pretended to be embarrassed. "But only once in a while!" They all turned away, hurried behind the shanty and roared with laughter that she wasn't supposed to hear.

÷

Everything quieted down. The fishermen went to fishing. She quit rubbing and threw her fishing line in the water. She felt wonderful. She'd started the morning out right for the old chauvinist fishermen. She'd seen past that silly stance, probably forced on them, into their good hearts and their scared souls that knew each of their karmic trips was almost up, that each one of them had one foot on a banana peel and the other in you-know-where. So, okay.

She sorted through each of the old men's personality traits with compassion and kindness, a lady bountiful until Jessup startled her out of her goody two shoes thinking with a bellow.

"Yew' gonna' stand there all day or ya' gonna' pull that feesh' in so's I can take it off the hook? We need ta' ketch' more fish."

She didn't ask him why they needed to catch more fish. She didn't care. She fished and watched the beautiful sunrise and listened to the men talking in low voices to each other about their health problems. George touched his chest and talked about his pacemaker and the fear he felt every time the tiniest bit of pressure or pain started in his chest. Barton talked about his blood pressure spiking without any known

154

reason. Orville talked about how his "nuts" had betrayed him, and Wade's circulation was severely restricted due to the name of something he couldn't pronounce.

She was glad she was able to take their minds off themselves for a few minutes with her shenanigans. And, she suspected, it was the first time they'd laughed in awhile. Their first laughs sounded like they were coming out of rusted tin cans tossed on a junk heap. Their laughs needed to be used more to loosen them up.

She knew Jessup wouldn't talk about anything wrong with him when she was near, and take a chance on her hearing it, because he was "sweet" on her. When she was around, he strode down the long walk to the dock like an action hero in a movie. The guys laughed at him for it, and he gave them baleful glares. They didn't say too much, though, because he was the only ride they had to go fishing or most anywhere else for that matter, and he tolerated their restrictions with patience.

Only Barton was allowed to drive anymore. She'd heard him talking mournfully to the others about his young wife making him move to Florida. He called it "The Rocking Chair State."

The next morning, she wore a plaid shirt buttoned wrong, the day after, her hair uncombed. She fished with them in the morning before the sun came up, while the air was still cool and sweet. She wore flashy sequined flip flops one morning. Jessup said he was afraid the fish would be blinded by them. She munched peanut butter sandwiches while leaning over the cool metal rails watching the water dancing easy below. The water lapping and the dove like murmurs of the men's tired voices formed a gentle, velvet background.

She listened to their soft, mournful stories of aging and their assessments of the inevitable toll it took on them and would keep on taking. She listened when they gathered into a bunch and fished near enough to her so she could hear their stories that no one else wanted to listen to any more. Everyone else had already heard them or was dead. They confided in her with their backs turned away. They pretended she couldn't hear them and in turn, she pretended she didn't hear them. It was a calm, watery confessional with gentle sunrise and a breeze as old as forgiveness and grace. This place was these old fisherman's church—their cathedral.

The old men talked about how they'd grown up together and about all the fishing spots they'd fished. She knew they'd miss Barton terribly when he moved to Florida. They'd known him for half a century or more; his wife hadn't walked the earth too long past that. They blamed it on his evil young wife, who was making him pull up roots and leave his best friends behind.

One morning when she got in the Bronco, she noticed the old men's energy levels were low. She started shivering and complaining about the cold. None of them offered her their shirt or a coat, but they perked up. All of them became interested and righteous. They conferred with each other over this new problem. Orville spoke for them.

"Ya' shoudda' brought somethin' heavier to ware! WE know how to dress right for the weather."

"None of ya' kin' spare a thing?"

"Ye'll jist' hafta suffer." Barton stated sadly.

"I don't wanna' suffer!" she whined.

"Jessup, gimme' yer' coat!" she ordered him in a loud whine.

He raised his eyebrows at her. "I took it out of the back yesterday."

"Where is it?" she asked in a sharp voice. He looked at her like she was stupid.

"It's at home. In the house. Not here."

She stared out the window and spoke angrily, "Humph! No gentlemen on this bus, I guess!"

There was just a slight hesitation before the guys in the back happily whisper-yelled, "Ya' got that right, sister! All we are is tough old fishermen!"

She heard the strength filling their voices, and smiled secretly in satisfaction.

As soon as they met Orville and Wade down on the dock, she shivered and complained again. George, Barton, and Jessup explained the problem to Orville and Wade all at the same time. Their voices rose and fell as she walked off, smiling to herself, took her rod and tackle box, efficiently baited her hook, and dropped it into the water.

The men finally broke up their huddle and walked over to her. Barton spoke for them again. Gravely he asked, "You want us to pitch in and buy ya' a little pink coat to keep you warm? It'll match them little pink boots we was gonna' git' ya' here while back."

The rest of the men standing behind him snickered. She frowned. "I do like pink," she conceded again in a grave voice, "… sometimes."

The men went to slapping their knees and guffawing as well as they were able.

÷

The mornings flew by. They all kept catching fish. Perch, catfish, croppies. She gave hers to Jessup. He took them home and cleaned and froze most of them, giving her a few fillets now and then. Then one morning on the way home, Jessup announced that they finally had enough frozen fish to hold another Saturday night fish dinner at the church in Alamoosa.

Saturday night was music night. Orville broke in and said he was supposed to sing that night. He hit a few practice notes and she cringed while everybody else murmured approval.

"You all gotta' be really hard of hearing," she muttered under her breath.

Jessup gave her a long look. She frowned back at him absently. She was thinking about where to buy ear plugs that weren't too noticeable.

Jessup said without taking his eyes off of her, "Orville, I'm savin' a fireball to give ya' jist' before you sing Saturday night." They all laughed.

'What's so funny?" she asked. Orville explained.

"There was this woman who sang every week that was sweet on Jessup, but he wasn't sweet on her! She sang him love songs every week from

158

the stage. Just like this."

Orville clasped his hands to his chest and made heaving motions, fluttered his lashes, rolled his eyes heavenward and simpered. Then he widened his eyes at Jessup and started to sing another Hank Williams nugget about lost love and ornery dogs. He stopped, caught his breath, and went on with his story.

"I guess Jessup finally had enough of his sweet thang' singin' ta' him. One night when she set down beside him like she allus' did before she went up on stage to sing, he didn't say a word, he just handed her a fireball. She took it and popped it right in her mouth, she was so pleased he'd finally given her something. In a minute, her face turned beet red. Her eyelashes started flappin', tears started flyin', and she went to drinking water as fast as she could.

Jessup popped a fireball into his own mouth and acted like nothing was going on. She didn't know Jessup could eat hell fire and not be bothered by it, so she must a' thought she was havin' some kind a' bad spell.

Well, about that time, they called her up on the stage. She staggered up there and cried and coughed and shouted her way through something she called a song. Most everybody thought she got saved 'cause the singing is held in the church anyway, so it was real convenient. Didn't hafta' go nowhere to git' it done. They was real happy for her!"

Jessup explained briefly. "Couldn't help myself." They all laughed. "Now, about the fish fry...Jist' about every three months, we've caught enough fish to put on a fish supper for the church. We fry the fish and layer 'em' in two big pans and carry them over to the church in Alamoosa for the Saturday night supper and sing-along. Other people bring the side dishes. The church is about thirty miles from here usin' back roads."

He grinned at her.

"Ya' wanna' go? Ya' kin' help fry the fish on Saturday afternoon before we take off. We'll need a couple of hours to do it."

He widened his large blue eyes at her.

"Okay," she said slowly, like he had just offered her one of those fireballs.

"You'll like it." Jessup said encouragingly.

"Maybe, maybe not." she answered.

She showed up on Saturday afternoon at Jessup's house to help fry the fish. Jessup was the only one there.

"Where's the rest of the guys?" she asked.

"Oh, I always do this part. They have to rest up for the trip," he said nonchalantly.

"I smell a trick here."

Jessup grinned at her and didn't answer. He handed her a stack of pictures of his deceased wife and a stack of the prize croppies he'd caught throughout his fishing career. The wife was always sleeping in the pictures, and the croppies were always fourteen inches long. Then he said he was lonely and looking for someone "to marry up with" since his wife died five years ago. He waggled his eyebrows at her. She looked at the sleeping woman in every picture. Had the poor woman been heavily medicated or bourbon'd, or had he bored her to death? She ignored his insinuations.

They began prepping the fish for the deep fryer. Now and then, she munched a sample of the steaming, golden, crispy pieces. "Yum!" she nodded at Jessup. "You sure can fry fish!"

He grinned back, pleased.

After several hours of fish frying in Jessup's small fryer, they were done. The fish repined in golden brown layers in two big silver pans. They covered them with foil. Touching her blouse, she said, "This stinks! It smells like fish! I can't go anywhere in it. I need to go home and change."

"Well, ya' better hurry, cause' we're runnin' late!" Jessup shouted. "Oh, hell. Women!...I'll pick up the guys and be right over to git' ya!'

They each grabbed up a pan of fish and carried it out to the back of Jessup's Bronco and loaded it in before they each rushed away on their errands.

She ran in her house and pulled on a blue sweater she found stored in a bag in the back of the closet. It was perfect for the cool evening weather. She was ready and waiting when Jessup pulled in the driveway.

She ran to the Bronco, jumped into the passenger side and slammed the door shut. Jessup turned and wheeled out into the quiet, tree lined street.

"Hey! This is gonna' be fun, guys!" she turned to smile at the guys in the back. Her eyes widened. Evidently, Jessup's vehicle was some sort of a mini-bus, as well as doubling for a faded green four wheeler. First of all, there were two seats back there, and not only that, they were filled with people! Her eyes ran over them. There was Barton, George, Orville, Wade, and a white haired, skinny old lady draped with a home knit pink shawl and a lovely smile.

She gaped as the woman smiled at her and said, "Hello."

"Jessup," the woman said, not taking her eyes off her. "You didn't tell this little gal that your Mom was going?"

"No ma'am," Jessup said carefully.

"And you didn't tell her that I've been waitin' ta' meet the gal my son talks about so much?"

"No ma'am," Jessup said, staring straight ahead as though his life depended on it. Even though the conversation was holding her in a stunned sort of fascination, something else was demanding her attention.

"Peee UUUUGH!" she shouted, jerking around to the front. She sniffed the arm of her sweater, then the front of it. Then she shoved her sleeved arm under Jessup's nose.

"Does this sweater stink?"

He sniffed.

"Oh my God, if it does, I don't have anything else to wear! I grabbed it out of a storage bag in the closet. The bag must have mothballs in it. Oh, no!"

"It smells just fine to me." Jessup said mildly. She jerked her arm back and sniffed it again. Her eyes began to water as the powerful smell of naphtha surrounded her like a deadly fog. She tried to ignore the smell and turned to the back seat again. She batted her eyes at the old lady in the back seat.

"How do you do?" she smiled sweetly at her. The old lady looked back at her with red, watery eyes.

She squinted at the little old lady. Was she crying? Did she hate her as soon as she saw her? Did she expect her to pledge her undying love to Jessup this instant so she could have her for a daughter-in- law? Was she mad or jealous because Jessup talked about her nonstop?

They stared at each other until the old lady finally sneezed and put a Kleenex to her eyes and declared, "My name is Miranda."

She barely heard her. Her attention was forced back to the awful smell permeating the Bronco. She jerked back around and sniffed her sleeves again.

Jessup said mildly, "Still smellin' somethin'?"

She noticed his eyes were turning red and watery, and that he had a disconcerting habit of speeding up real fast, then slowing down real fast.

"Why are you driving like this?" she asked.

"It's mother's blood pressure." He stated matter of factly, as though his words explained everything.

"What's that got to do with it?"

"When she taps me on the shoulder, I slow down. That means her blood pressure is high. I speed up when it gets low."

She glanced out at the gravel road they were traveling. He was speeding like a race car driver. Dust was flowing like a river around them.

"So I can take it to mean her blood pressure's low right now?"

Jessup nodded.

She heard several of the old men coughing in the back seat and turned towards them.

George was coughing and tapping his chest,

Barton and Orville were searching in their pockets for pills.

"Okay..." she muttered to herself. "Something is bad wrong. There's a stench that could down a bull loose in this vehicle and I am out in the boonies with a bunch of loonies. It's almost dark and I forgot my cell phone. I have no clue where I am, and the old lady is pale and panting, and George seems to have passed out. Great!"

Just then Orville started singing. He wailed and screeched through an old church song, something about no matter where you are Jesus will find you, while Jessup stopped and started and flew and lurched down the gravel road, jumping from forty miles per hour to eighty with the old lady clutching her head and tapping him on the shoulder from time to time.

The horrible smell became overpowering. She rolled down the window and sucked in the dusty air and stared out into the dusk closing in fast around the vehicle.

"Breathe!" she ordered herself.

She had just decided it was worth it to jump from the vehicle, abandoning all within, taking her chances on becoming disguised meat road kill, when they shot across a street and lurched to a sudden stop in a paved parking lot.

'This here's the church." Jessup said by way of explanation. By that time, all of the windows were down. The horrible stench was rolling out of them.

For a couple seconds, she felt like she'd been zapped back to earth from a bad trip through the Twilight Zone. Then she realized with mounting horror that she'd have to go through the reek again going home unless she could figure out where the stench was coming from.

She jumped out of the Bronco and ran up and down, waving her arms to air out her sweater so she would know if that's what stunk so bad. Across the street lurked a tiny gas station. All little towns had them. She nodded to herself and reasoned that most of them sold T-shirts to people who wanted something to wear home that didn't have somebody else's smell on it. Love in the boondocks.

A couple minutes later she realized it wasn't her sweater that stunk. Everybody else had fled the Bronco and were walking up and down as fast as they could. All the Bronco doors stood open. The smell was coming from inside of it. Maybe it wasn't the polite thing to do, but she HAD to find where the stench was coming from. She couldn't possibly survive a ride home immersed in it.

She peered into the Bronco. Jessup sighed and watched her. Finally he conceded, "Well, I DID put two teeny tiny, itty bitty little round containers of deodorizer under the back seat before I picked everybody up."

She scowled at him and stood back, hands on hips, tapping her feet.

"Well, Mister, I think you better get in there and get them out!"

Jessup was a bossy man, one who didn't take orders. She'd never heard him laugh anything close to a full belly laugh. She didn't care. She put one hand on her hip, tapped her foot again, pointing to the Bronco. Miranda and the old men stood there, watching.

He glanced at her guiltily, ambled to the back doors of the Bronco, and pulled out two tiny round discs filled with something that looked like salve. He held them out for her to look at like a little boy whose hands needed washing. She sniffed them.

"Oh my God! EEUUUghhh!! Where did you get those? They're like the nuclear waste in really bad "B" movies! They're probably alive or something! And I bet we don't have any atomic waste containers in this ratty little god forsaken burg!"

"I got em' two for a dollar at a gas station just like that one," he explained mildly as he pointed across the street. "I thought they would make the Bronco smell better."

"Oh, really? I'm surprised any of us have any hair left! Or life! And did you check to see where they were made? In some third world country whose only aim in life is to kill off bad, rich Americans using fake deodorizers that choke them to death while they ride around in their Broncos? Or were they made by aliens using abundant, fragrant green cesspool petroleum to kill off humans?"

He examined the writing on one of them. "It says made in Gopie."

Jessup leaned over and laid the two silver containers underneath the Bronco.

"Oh no, you don't! Those damn things will peel the paint right off your Bronco! By the time we head home, it'll be nothing but a big pile of rust, and maybe worse! Give em' to me!" she ordered. Jessup meekly handed them over.

Suddenly, he started laughing. He laughed until he was holding his sides and wiping his eyes.

His mother stepped up to her. "That's the first time I've heard him laugh like that in years! Thank you, girl, you are so good for him!"

She ignored his mother's soulful words. Somehow she knew they were the prequel to a proposal. Lord knows she'd been there before, and she intended to cut that little scenario short. She threw the tiny troublesome discs into the weed choked vacant lot across the street. Then she whirled and covered her ears. Nothing happened. She took her hands down. "I thought they might explode!' she explained. The smell was finally leaving. She took a deep breath of the untainted country air. "Ohhh!" she said in relief.

Jessup snickered. He took her arm and she let him. They strolled to the back of the bronco. He jauntily picked up one foil covered pan and she lifted the other. Miranda, held up by Orville, followed them to the church. Orville practiced a few notes of his song. George's walker gleamed silver in the setting sun. Barton and George leaned on it. She watched Wade amble left, then right.

She sighed, turned to Jessup and smiled. He was watching her. The decision she thought would take so long, had only taken a few seconds.

She noticed how blue his eyes were and how they twinkled. She thought about how their unspoken thoughts played so well off each other as they turned in unison to carry the foil covered pans of fried fish into the church for the

Alamoosa Saturday night sing-along and fish
supper.

12.   Aluminum Foil

When I was thirty five, I got a hysterectomy and was lucky to be left alive. That crap doctor didn't believe in any kind of hormone therapy, HRT's, (Hormone Replacement Therapy) so he didn't tell me it existed.

I got shoved straight into hell in an instant. Forced into a headlong rush of middle-aged diminished capacity insanity from lack of hormones in one single instant. My body went nuts, along with my mind and a few other parts. It struck me like lightning, frying me a new asshole. I became one, too. An asshole. Fried, burnt, crispy, and baked, I began to function on what quickly got down to three out of ten cylinders. I became a crazed, mean asshole to everyone I encountered. Yep. My whole life changed to Crap on Wheels with just one stroke of that crap doctors knife.

My mind and body reacted by falling headlong into a screaming well of nameless, constant fear A.H. (After Hysterectomy) from lack of hormones, while my suffering body turned my hair from brown to gray, then used alternating currents A.C.D.C. to turn it screaming white, with thin with strands floating up like electric wiring from my scalp. I went from brown to dancing white electrodes within three months. Remember I was thirty five when this happened. I looked like Albert you know who, like I'd stuck my finger in a light socket, and it was stuck there forever.

I dragged myself into that crap doctors office over and over, (AH) asking him to find out what was wrong with me and fix it, but that sorry assed crap doctor still wouldn't offer me even one teensy bit of hormones to help me survive the madness, the insanity of the soul he'd caused my life to be thrown into. He'd let me die first.

Idiotically, I stayed in my role as the village idiot. I assumed that crap doctor knew everything, so I didn't get a second opinion before or after the surgical event that threw my life into a living hell.

That crap doctor didn't believe in hormones for me. No, that's not quite accurate—he believed in DIY hormones, the kind our bodies churn out day-by-day. He just didn't believe in "store bought" (HRT) hormones, you see, and didn't mention them to me as a merciful option A.H. (After Hysterectomy) until eight years later. He wouldn't have offered them then, he would have let me die, and I would have let him, except for his wife.

I'll never forget when the miracle took place. It was right after his wife's bird nest fell, and she told him she *would* have those hormones (HRT)and he could go to hell. She shouted this right in front of a roomful of dozing patients including dumbass me. Yeah, wake up calls come in a lot of different ways. Thank god I got one.

She swore she wasn't going to suffer like she'd seen his female patients suffer, including me. She pointed at me with her finger. I said, "Who, what? What hormones?"

She looked at me with pity. Then that crap doctor patted her on the head and said he'd read real research showing that female hormones would turn her into a sex-crazed maniac, and he didn't think he could keep up with that kind of stuff. He said, to put a fancy cap on it, neither he nor all the other guys he'd saved from a bad sex fate by not giving their wives hormones could keep up with that stuff, except maybe a little of that stuff would go well if their golf scores got low.

She ignored his sorry ass and got hormones from a lady doctor and left her fancy crap doctor husband to screw himself.

But meanwhile...

There's me. I sat in his crappy office with the fake plants and dust, thinking hard. I'd set up most every black, evil, dreadful, sinful, night without those hormones to give me relief, because I didn't know about them. What a dumbass I was! I'd slept a little bit during the days and died every night a thousand different ways until that final fateful appointment with Doctor Craphead....when his wife spilled the beans.

Eight years it was to the day, when she spilled the beans...eight years of him evading the horror he'd surgically introduced into the life that used to be mine.

Grimly I dragged myself onto his examining table that day for about the 500th. time, wearing that split gown disposable thing, thinking about what Craphead Doctors little wifey had said. Things were gonna' be different this time.

I lay there, gasping, gray and sweaty, stinking

of ozone and exuding Snickers bar breath. I ate sweets so I could keep going in survival mode and avoid any more lightning strikes. Snickers, my gray asshole was safe from getting singed; no Snickers, my asshole and bereft womb became the prime target of lightning-frying. I was a whispering old asshole crone at home, a battle worn, acid wrinkled wicked crone, almost bald, bent over. I was forty three now. I was thirty five when I went under the knife. I'd survived hell so far but with big prices. So had my family. Now I lived with an alienated family who believed I was crazy, bat shit crazy, unbelievably, awfully, miserably, mean crazy! And I was.

Well Craphead doctor came in and I fixed him with a glare and suddenly that crap doctor's light bulb finally came on. It came on while I was clutching that paper gown around myself up there on his examining table that day. I grimly watched the light bulb above his head, naked, hanging down on a thin electric wire. I watched his fevered, obnoxious brain light it up at last. I never said a word but the room reeked with my unsaid rage. Quickly Craphead doctor gave me the tests I'd needed forever, then acted surprised when he "discovered" I was in serious, death defying, alligator wrestling,(skin) all over atrophy from lack of hormones.

After a first hasty shot in my rear end, a golden-hued blue shot thick with rich hormones, surprised lightning struck my sorry asshole self, and I almost fainted. I thought to myself, I don't know how many times this damned lightning has to strike my sorry asshole and those parts now residing in the unknown just above it, but I hope it quits pretty damn soon! Craphead doctor left the room in a hurry. I pulled my pants up and stole a box of his nurses purple examination gloves on the way out. I didn't know why at the time, but I found out later. Thank god my unconscious didn't get fried (AH)! I took the gloves home and stashed them under things in a dresser drawer.

It took time, but I almost became human again, as if a Melting Frankenstein Woman could ever qualify as human again in any universe.

I got one hormone shot a month. Then I switched to daily tablets. I was a dumbass, a fried dumbass by not figuring it out years ago.

So you think that's where my story ends, like leftover Spam? No. You're not that lucky, just like I wasn't that lucky.

I started on the hormones, but I had to catch up. I slept fourteen hours a night, snoring and dreaming, making up for lost time. In my dreams, I carried giant jars of glowing hormones around from place to place, hiding them in secret places so I would have them to take for the rest of my life. In my dreams, I was no longer a dowdy, frumpy, silent or screaming, a no in between, womb-less woman.

I slowly began to hope that things might right themselves in my world again, at least some of it. I groped my way along, trying to put my life back together like the unseen but intuited pieces of a 1,000-piece picture puzzle of a puddle of milk spilled in fresh snow, with mostly no borders.

First I stood up straight. Then I got my hair back. So what if it was white now? Who cared if my persona included wrinkled skin, (alligator)a voice that scraped and rasped like a rusty, dented fender making people wince, and a goatee on my chin I kept forgetting to shave? I welcomed all of it. My animal totem became the buzzard. A dirty, stinking, used life is better than none, so I hugged it close and avoided all the hair removal products in the grocery store.

I felt pretty damn delicate and almost cute for a few hours after each hormone dose. A flawed new beginning, granted, but I didn't have to leave home anymore to try to find some damn meaning to the Hell I'd lived in for years. No more traveling to some God forsaken reservation in Hellsville or to a Waffle House one suburb over in Hellacious.

I had been frazzled, fried, shaked and baked B.S. (Before Shots). All I was able to do was drive, drive, drive all night long. Now all I needed to do was take the hormones and keep my sorry ass to home. I now had the hormonal rain to ease the tremors and quakes and to settle me, myself, and I down.

But there was a score I needed to settle first. I took the stolen purple nurses examination gloves out of the dresser drawer and placed them in my desk drawer. Yes, I was once a writer. Before the surgical event. Today, I would begin my career in writing again. Whatever it took. I researched. Then I put the gloves on. I sent newspaper clippings. Then one page letters I hired written by various drunken vagrants downtown. Then receipts I picked up off streets, and pages from that famous author of death and mayhem, Poe. I sent until the glove supply ran out. I felt finished with my part at that point, and complete when Craphead doctor and his family suddenly relocated to Arizona. He didn't leave a forwarding address or refer his patients to other doctors. He just plain left.

The hormones ignored my realizations and vengeance and helped me anyway. They ignored me and moved forward, healing the places where my blood and bone was torn to ribbons and shreds before I ever got started good on life. They released stalwart goodness into my system, a little too late, but they did it anyway. I realized what a sucker I was for taking too long to find out when somebody was tricking me, like that Craphead doctor.

I'm not offering excuses. I don't have any. There's other dumbass people like me who stumble and fall all through life. They start out that way and it never ends.

These days, I can give a short history that will never change. Nothing I can do to make it change now. I can say, "Well, my husband left me anyway and I didn't blame him and helped him go. Then my boy followed him for a while, and I didn't blame him either."

And how many times have you heard this one?

"Yeah, my daughter.. well... she had my first grandchild and life could have gone on, but I'd been a busted up unit too long, a Frankenstein woman, ignorant and barren with only two week old leftover kung pao to share with anyone. I was always too damn too late to make it up to them. I just didn't know it at the time.

I lost them all, and it killed me. I'm deader than a doornail. It has to be at God's insistence that I'm still alive, not mine, an aged, wrinkled, creeping piece of junk sound, crying, wailing, bitching forever, living in loneliness and sorrow, watching Godzilla and Ray Man movies.

Nowadays, what's left of me is like a piece of aluminum foil, full of creases and wrinkles and stains. The kind of tough, multipurpose, reduce, reuse, recycled foil that, no matter how much you smooth it out, the wrinkles stay until it finally gets so thin and brittle you have to throw it away. It just never goes away; it never becomes, it's always been that way, yeah, right from the start.

13.   The Parrot and Joe's Mom

The church was filled with masses of flowers and solemn, quiet people. Most of them smelled good, with a few flagrantly bourbon. The priest stood tall and proud in front of them, an open Bible in his large hands. Dressed in black robes, he was giving the eulogy for the woman who'd lived across the street from the church for the last fifty years. He snuck a look at his watch. He hoped he could pull off the eulogy and get away in time to watch his favorite sports team take the field. He expected to; this one should be easy.

The priest had been assigned to the church for the last ten years. He spoke of the woman's strong faith and devotion. He talked about how she sat on her front porch in her housecoat and slippers every day come rain or shine, praying from ten o'clock in the morning until two in the afternoon, while she stared across the street at the front doors of the church.

He said the church had been blessed by her diligent prayers. He said he saw her sitting on her porch and praying every day from his office window. He said he watched her staring across the street, praying out loud as she counted her rosary beads and perpetually, even religiously, smoked her many cigarettes. He said he only caught the sound of her voice, not her words, but he was sure of her constant prayers. He said she tossed her cigarette butts in a bucket with "Butts Brocket" emblazoned on it by a person who could print neatly on galvanized metal but could not spell worth sheet cake. No one laughed at his little joke.

The priest cast his eyes upward and said the woman's devotion had given him great encouragement in his serving of God. In fact, he often asked himself, how could he be weary when such belief and faith were shown to him every day in the faithful woman sitting across the street?

He said for at least three of the last ten years of her life she carried a large, multi-hued parrot out on the porch with her each morning, placing it carefully on a perch someone built for the big bird. The parrot talked and squawked and whistled while she prayed.

Then the priest smiled. He said he liked to think the woman had been a good influence on the bird. That was the padre's way of making another small joke; one so puny that it fell, like a molted feather, silent and small into the hollow silence of the mourners and the family sitting stiffly on the hard, polished, wooden pews in the front row. No one smiled back.

The priest wound up for his big finish. He believed none of his parishioners knew what he was about to reveal. He leaned forward and said that he'd crossed the street a few times to visit the woman and pray with her. He said she was a faithful wife to her husband, a good mother to her three sons, and a fine member of the church. He said he missed her presence on the porch the last couple of years while she was battling her lengthy illness. (He was wrong; everybody knew that. Whose genuflected knee was he trying to pull?)

And now she was here, at rest in the church she attended for more than fifty years. Her life had come full circle. It was complete.

When the priest offered the funeral mass and held up the communion wafer, no one went forward to take it except the woman's skinny, aged, dapper little husband. A look of surprise came over the priest's face when no one else got up and walked to the front of the church.

The priest grew quiet, nearly all the rites were resolved. The funeral proceeded with more prayers and flicked drops of holy water. At last, the old woman was laid in her final resting place. An old maple tree stood near her grave. A tender blanket of fresh, sprouting spring grass rippled around the maple tree's roots. The priest hurried away. He was just a few minutes away from watching his sports team start their playoffs.

Later, back at the old woman's house, the dinner for the mourners was served. The new girlfriend of Joe, the second son, asked him about his mother sitting on the front porch all those years. It seemed sort of psychotic to the girlfriend who was busy taking freshman courses in psychology at college.

She'd watched the stiff, guarded masks come over the three sons and the father's faces while the priest was giving the eulogy and she wondered why.

Joe was her latest boyfriend. She'd flown back to his hometown with him for the funeral. He turned to her and sighed. Then he recited his answer in a flat monotone without any inflection or feeling. He said that ten years ago his mother stole three hundred thousand dollars, all of their shared inheritance from his father's only brother. No one ever found out what she did with the money.

The inheritance came from his father's family, and when his father received it, he simply put it in the bank until he could decide how to invest it.

His father's relationship with his mother changed from the day he found out she went to the bank and drew out all the inheritance money. There was nothing to show for it, not a thing, the son told his girlfriend. It was as though it disappeared into thin air.

His father railed at his mother in grief and guttural incredulity. Nothing he said or did moved her sufficiently to tell him where the cash was. She left him no alternative. There was no remaining thread of a reason for him to refrain in any way from becoming mean to her and ignoring her.

The old woman stubbornly kept her secret, but lost all of them in the doing of it. All three of the boys moved away, and their father spent most of his time staying away from wherever his purse-lipped wife was at.

She went to her grave not telling anyone what she did with the money. Instead of confessing, she sat on the front porch each morning in a rocking chair, staring at the mail box in front of the house. It stood outside the fence, directly in line with the priest's office window in the church across the street.

She spent her time on the front porch

smoking and praying, cussing and smoking, and smoking some more while waiting for the mailman who delivered the mail each day between ten and two thirty. Each day she waited for him to bring her the *Publisher's Sweepstakes* money she believed she would win.

And the bird? Well, that tubby old parrot cussed just like she always did. As soon as the old woman began her final descent into her long illness, her irritated husband and resentful sons gave the parrot away. The old woman couldn't talk to anyone anymore. If she couldn't talk, who would the parrot converse with?

The sun sank, casting red rays across the old woman's front porch. People glanced at their watches while they ate every bite of the catered food at the post-funeral gathering. Proper etiquette deemed it inappropriate to speak of any other subject but the dead woman. Conversations were short, revealing nothing new nor long-hidden in the skeleton's closet, finally freed for the tongue clucking.

Joe's girlfriend found herself alone, stubbing out her cigarette on the old woman's front porch. She pitched the butt into the Butts Brocket bucket, where years of the old woman's non-filtered butts lay clotted, rotting like snuffed out dreams.

14.   Apple Jelly

I made apple jelly the other morning for the first time. It turned out just the color of Flower Woman's hair. I held a jar of its sweetness up to the light to examine the red-gold color better. Next thing you know, I was crying and looking through old picture albums.

There she was, posing nonchalantly with a mischievous, undaunted by life smile, thick, curling, red gold hair framing her face, her big, earthy goddess body unabashedly on display for the camera.

I stood beside her, skinny and stiff and grinning because I was with her, my fine, short brown hair sticking every which way, the only wild thing about me, she always said.

She never gave a damn that she was overweight and middle aged and life had passed her by because she hadn't been married in twenty years, and her kids were all off living in exotic places, and she didn't have life insurance or a house or money to leave them, let alone one to live in. Only an inheritance of a sort of freedom they didn't choose because they didn't understand it.

Flower Woman. That's what she was called back in the sixties when she was a devoted flower child—a hippie. She lived in the sun, smiling and trail blazing, while I lived in the shadows of propriety and duty, making sure I kept a husband and children and plenty of work to do.

When all of that got torn away from me by time and life, I stepped beyond myself and found her. She rushed into my life and pulled it apart and laughed at it while I stood there, holding the threads of my past life, mourning its ending endlessly. I would have gone to my grave in that condition if she hadn't pranced into my life and pinched me out of my spell. It hurt, too.

"Waa! Waa!" she'd said. "Big baby! Nobody has that much time left!"

She clowned and cajoled and capered until I threw the rest of the faded threads into the air, letting them fall where they might. I ran away with her, afraid they might land before I got the chance to change, to be different, to have fun at last.

Oh, the times we had! Four years worth before I got pulled back into my duties, turning my back on her pleading and anger and friendship, not crying when she left to go live in the Rocky Mountains, sick with heart trouble that was more than physical.

I closed the album and put it back underneath the stack of albums holding my father, mother, husband's, and children's pictures. I put her last. That time was over.

I got up and went to the kitchen to row the still warm apple jelly jars evenly on a pantry shelf. Then I stood back and admired them. It was the first batch of jelly I ever made, and it turned out perfect.

I have never liked jellies, just jams. I don't like the texture of jelly, you see, all smooth and too easy.

But I think I'm going to make some more of it

anyway. I can just taste it when it's dark and cold this winter, clear red and gold, like sunshine, and sweet, so sweet, spread smooth on a hot slice of my homemade bread.

15.   The Statue in the Hall

She sat in grim silence at the long, expensive table. He sat sideways in the dusky light at the other end of the table, posing so she could feast her eyes on him. He'd called her to him again, thoughtlessly breaking into her family routine, and she went to him without fail and without question, like she always did.

She turned her head slightly until they were both staring through the flawless, off white designer blinds covering the dining room windows. Strategically and partially closed, the blinds discreetly muted a neighbor's colorful Christmas lights, lights blinking a hopeful, secret code through perfectly correct white slats.

She blinked, turned away and glanced around. The room was all whites and angular lines, except for the light gray designer carpet cut close and tight to the floor. The table they sat at was an antiseptic, long, thin rectangle of black glass from Paris. The chairs around it were cold silver chrome, laced with stiff black leather, designed especially for him by a famous New York architect.

He relaxed, not speaking, lounging back into his chair at the head of the table. He neither knew nor cared that the table cost the equivalent of a year's wages and more in many parts of the world. He sat at the table, posing as if he were one of Michelangelo's beautiful sculptures, as if he knew her greatest need was to bask in his beauty. Oh, he knew her so well!

He leaned back in his chrome and black chair, crossing his feet at his ankles, resting in suave indifference and complete self-confidence. He knew well the power of beauty, particularly his own. His life was dedicated to it. He knew, but didn't care the cost of it to others or himself.

He had many social acquaintances but no wives or children or close friends. Just relatives who faked a respectable fondness while maintaining the correct reserve.

She examined his reflection in the large, frameless, square mirror on the wall behind him. Her eyes wandered over his short gray hair and the seams in his neck, and the roundness of the backs of his ears. She thought they looked like two outer rings of giant, pink teardrops in the dusky light.

She knew he was aware of his reflection in the mirror, that she was looking at him, trapped by his beauty. It was the place they always met. Everything fit him impeccably, from his many pairs of shoes to his tuxedo, suits, ties, and trendy, carefully-creased jeans. Even when he was once poor, the prince-to-be sitting in front of her always kept his clothes clean, neat, and perfect for all occasions.

His hair was cut just right, and he kept it in place with a few discreet spritzes of a men's salon hairspray. His thick, straight hair was a deep shade of brown when she first met him. His eyes were the same shade of brown. He always knew the right thing to say. He escorted her to museums and art shows and once, to the opera. He chose her clothes, showed off his hair, his eyes, his clothing, and lastly, her, the woman he'd selected for this event.

She sat almost at the other end of the long table as though removing herself from his presence. She sat there by habit in the place he was comfortable with her being in. Over time, she'd moved from chair to chair, first beside him, then down towards the end of the table. Love from a distance.

÷

She waited for him to explain why he'd called her, but knew he wouldn't. He never did. Now she knew his call was an excuse. He needed someone to admire him, and it was her turn. He fed off it.

Her lips formed a thin drop of a fleeting smile. She didn't know if it would be followed by tears. He had no way of knowing this time was different, but she knew it on all levels.

She must not be hasty. This needed to be done right. These next few minutes needed to have their own kind of beauty, for she was a prisoner of that need, trapped in it in her own way, always would be, just as he was.

They were both artists. She was self-taught and came to it late in life, awed by the pleasure and power of it. She enjoyed the steady, small successes she achieved, but they were secondary to the relief, fun, and passionate spontaneity she breathed in when she worked.

Of course, he'd trained for years all over the world. He made his living as a clothing designer who loved architecture and museums and knew the right words to say about all paintings and sculptures. He was the only man she'd ever known who could do that. He loved and collected household objects, assigning meanings to them that went far beyond their utilitarian uses.

She watched him handling objects of art with intensity, gentleness, and rapt attention, shutting everything else out. She began thinking about him handling her the same way. She translated his knowledge of things to mean he himself owned depth and passion, but she'd been completely wrong. She thought he'd understand that she'd felt like a household object too many years, unappreciated, stuck in a drawer no one every opened, used without understanding.

She was awed and fascinated by him; she grew to love him and it caused her to reject everyone else, family and all, in her yearning, her need for him to notice her. At night, before she got in bed to lay beside her sleeping husband, she thought of his long fingers running over the curves of her.

But while she waited like a doll on a shelf for him to discover her, without realizing it, she set out on a journey of self discovery. She ran her hands over her aging skin and felt it smooth out and cover the angular, skinny child she once was. She felt the blossoming curves and moist, sweet smell of her skin and red hair at seventeen.

Sometimes she studied her feet, remembering all the places they'd walked, and her hands, and all the things they'd handled. She studied them, remembering the sunlit barn of childhood when she stroked a cows nose. She recalled the rough bark on trees, and the silky green grass she lay upon. She numbered the sweet, new pink babies she'd held, their lungs moving in and out rapidly with first breaths fanning across her steady, capable, willing hands. She recalled frosty morning air and the scraping of windshields, fingers burning with fiery ice. Those hands in warmer times had molded clay and made cakes and explored a man's warm body on dark, sweet nights.

As she redefined herself, her forgotten passion and appreciation for living, breathing, moving life rose in her again. She became pretty in a new way. She was happy with the newness, yet a part of her still clung stubbornly to the belief that only *he* carried the magic she required to be truly happy, that only *he* could set her free.

÷

But time passed, and her journey was alone, and it was good. At last she realized her life never really included him. He was a beginning, a beautiful, distant doorway she'd stepped through to regain her forgotten capacity for life, joyful fun, and laughter.

She realized that he'd known all along about her hidden adoration for him. She stayed astounded, confounded and vexed at her secret discovery until she accepted that he loved her, as much as he could love anyone. He became a teacher and a gift giver to her.

She kept up the pretense for awhile, knowing it couldn't last. She never spoke to him of the cold, polite Ice King, a pretender to the throne, she now knew he was. Teachers always leave. Or the student leaves. Never matters what the subject is.

It would be a relief to give up the Ice King, to be set free to go home and get warm. Like flinging off an ice cape, she needed to step away from the cold so she could feel the heat and passion of life again with others. He stood in the way of eager arms surrounding her, holding her, everything she now longed for. Still, she loved him and always would.

÷

She sighed, settled back into her chair and turned to face him. He didn't return her gaze. She knew he wouldn't, because he needed to stay just as he was. There were other students waiting to take his classes. She gazed at him. He still thought allowing her to look upon the terrible beauty of him would stay irresistible, forever enough for her.

She smiled a cold, thin, purposeful smile. She stared down at her hands and flexed her long, sensitive fingers before she raised her head and looked through the blinds at the colorful Christmas lights.

The room stayed warm, dusky, and silent, waiting. She drew a long breath and began to pour the words she needed to say to set herself free into the waiting silence.

÷

190

"In grade school, I attended a new style of school, one with long, wide halls running alongside open classrooms. Each classroom was divided by a front and back wall and an outer wall of windows. Instead of a fourth wall with a door, there were bathrooms and a door to the outside for each classroom across a wide hall.

The school rooms were designed much like the cubicles many offices use these days. Naturally, the result was that all the teachers had to do double duty to keep their students quiet so that they did not disturb any of the other open classrooms and teachers.

The teachers were severe in their endeavors to keep us quiet, and to teach us. The only time any of us made any noise was when answering the teacher or after we were let out for recess on the playground.

I was fine with the situation. I was an excellent student and loved books from early on. I was terribly shy and very quiet and kept to myself. No one could bully me successfully or make me angry or cry. Nothing touched me. I was filled with ice and satisfied with myself and the internal arrangements I'd made to endure life. The shuffle of other children's feet going to or coming from the cafeteria or the gym or playground or to the bus did not affect me in any way.

Then one day, the classes on my side of the school were returning to our rooms from the cafeteria. The only noise was of our feet shuffling along the wide corridor running past the open classrooms.

I expected everything to be the same as always, but then, I looked down the long hallway and saw a statue of a white angel. I couldn't believe what I was seeing. She was small and gorgeous and stood on a pedestal of some kind. I couldn't take my eyes off her. I wondered how she got in the school, and if they knew she was there. Would they take her away? There had never been anything like her in my world before!"

She waited, giving him the chance to speak or at least look at her. It might have changed everything. But he didn't. He stayed motionless, staring out the window. She'd experienced his repulsion with emotions before.

She spoke into the silence again.

"The closer I came to the angel, for that is what she was, the more awed and dumbfounded I became. I began to cry without realizing it. In the dreary silence of the shuffling feet around me, I made joyful exclamations to her. My heart was full. I could not stop what was between us. No one around me mattered anymore. Just the statue in the hall.

"A new Beauty had entered my world. There was only us two in it. I wasn't alone any more. The lines of her are etched into my mind's eye to this day. She had reached the icy heart of me and thawed it out in one instant. Later, I learned that the angel was a statue on loan from a European museum. She was touring schools in the United States to awaken the young people to art and its meaning.

Another time, a famous violinist came to the school and played for us, and I heard and felt the wonder of the finest of live classical music for the first time. He was an incredible master of his instrument; through his playing, a love of music entered my soul, thawed it out and never left. There were more things, infrequently, but the miracle had happened. Those additions built upon my new awareness. I became alive to objects, to art, to music and in time, I also came to know they were neither human and alive, nor warm and with voices. I realized it was time to move on."

She looked around the room a final time. She didn't expect an answer. The room slowly filled with frigid emptiness.

÷

In a soft, firm voice she said, "The thing is, you always knew that my meeting you was like me seeing that statue in the hall. You also knew the price I would pay. That I would spend every night waiting, chilled, hopeful, alone in my soul, rejecting the love, affection and warmth offered by my husband and children and family. You knew it, and you didn't feel guilty or remorseful about it."

She stood up and placed her fingertips on his perfect table, marring its pristine surface. "I know now that is because you are an ice Prince. So of course you thought it moral, ethical, and fine for me to pay the prices needed. I'm not the first woman to follow you into your frozen hollowness, into your icy emptiness, and dwell

193

there far too long, waiting for you to grow warm. Many other fine women have met you and lost precious time. Time they'll never get back to experience the beauty of joy and affection from the warm and caring people in their lives. I'm taking my soul home now, back to the hearth, back to the place where life and love and warmth have been waiting for me all this time!"

She ran her fingers over the burled edge of the table, smearing it like a toddler with finger paints and said, "Our time was never ours. We never shared it. It belonged to the Muse. My price has been paid, and I hope to God I'm finished with you."

She swept her hand out, breathed in and out rapidly and said, "I'm so very lucky that I have time left! I must hurry, for I'll never waste another minute of it here with you. The cost is too high."

He didn't move or speak as she grabbed her coat and strode toward the door, not looking back. The door slammed shut behind her.

Silence settled into the room. Two single tears rolled slowly and carefully down his cheeks, just in the right place, just in the right way. A bright pink color trailed each tear, a pink acid, softly, silently etching a path down his white marble face as he resumed watching the Christmas lights blinking through the perfectly angled white wood slats on the windows.

16.   The Wedding Curtain

My sister Charlene was ten when I was born. Charlene was tall and thin, and I forever thought she was beautiful. Mama said she was crazy though, and we needed to hide the matches from her because she was a fire bug.

A pyro-maniac. Mama said any kind of a maniac was a dangerous animal. She said maniacs were wild and would hurt you, but the main thing was, you could never tell what they were gonna' do next, and so you must humor them and protect yourself from them.

I listened to the words Mama said, because she said them over and over again whenever Charlene was around. Her words owned a rhythm, like a song, and I found myself going over them again and again, like Mama did. Except I didn't know what they meant. I was too young. I wondered why Mama said that about Charlene and didn't say anything about our father being a drunkard maniac. He'd been gone awhile.

Charlene looked like him. Charlene's face was pale and thin with high cheek bones and sky blue eyes. I liked to touch her thin, straight hair, but didn't get to very often. It was fine and dark yellow, the color of clover honey mixed with ripe wheat. I knew she liked me because the scared, mean look left her face every time she looked at me.

My first strong memory of Charlene was when I was around five years old. Charlene and I were in the living room of the old house we lived in. Nobody else was in there, just her and me. She smiled her big wide smile at me as I sat on the floor watching her. Then she reached somewhere, and all of a sudden, there was a big box of Ohio Blue Tip matches in her hand. I thought it was magic when she grinned at me and struck a match on the side of the box. The fire from the match tip flared up, and I grinned at the acrid smell of it and the blue and yellow flame. I liked it.

Then Charlene strolled over to the one window in our living room. The window sat proud and crooked in the crumbling lathe board wall. Mama's one pink cotton lace curtain hung over it. Mama loved her pink lace curtain. I'd made a habit of spending my time sitting on the bare, faded wood of the living room floor looking at the patterns and color of Mama's pink lace curtain. It was the only pretty thing in the house besides Charlene and Mama, and I was fascinated by it.

Charlene struck another match, rolled her eyes at me and grinned, then held the match to the hem of the curtain. The pink lace started smoking, and a little flame started running across the hem.

She kept grinning at me. I wanted to tell her to stop because I didn't want the pink curtain to leave. The smell of the smoking curtain curled through the living room. Mama smelled it from the kitchen and came running and put the fire out. She hollered at Charlene, but Charlene just laughed and ran out the front door and down the porch steps. I listened to the sound of

Charlene's bare feet whispering swiftly down the rickety, silvered steps, like a ghost, like she hadn't ever been here with us.

Mama took the curtain down and shortened the hem with scissors. Then she sewed the hem back together with a needle and thread and hung the curtain back up over the window.

A few weeks after Charlene burned part of the curtain, some of Mama's people came from some place far away to visit her. Everyone living around us on the dusty old gravel road had electricity, but there was none in our house. It was too old and shabby to carry it, and the landlord was afraid of the house burning down if he tried to put it in. We used kerosene lamps at night, and we had an ancient wood burning stove standing in the middle of the living room floor to heat the old place in the winter.

There was never much food, but Mama was proud. She took the pink lace curtain down and washed it and ironed it. She spread it out over the old beat up table in the kitchen and it looked real pretty. Then she served the best fried chicken and mashed potatoes and biscuits to our company on it, right in the middle of the day.

Mama's people left about the time the sun set. When they were gone, Mama took the pink lace curtain off of the table, shook it out good, and tacked it back up over the window.

Things went along like they always did, like Mama's green runner beans slow climbing the corn stalks out back, and then one day, Charlene told Mama she was gonna' to run off and get married. I listened to her and Mama quarreling for days before Charlene took off.

The morning after she left, I was sitting in the living room, watching the sun mollies float through the air. I heard Mama moping around in the kitchen, cryin' a little bit here and there. Then she come in the living room and stared at the pink lace curtain awhile. Then she took it down and carried it over to the treadle sewing machine in the corner and set down with it. I watched her studying it while she set there, her back to the room, stooped over the sewing machine for privacy. She run her hands over the curtain, smoothing every inch of it, again and again. I thought she might wear it out before she got done.

The warm sunlight fell across her where she sat. She was so beautiful, but I knew even way back then, that I couldn't ever have her be mine, not even for a minute. Nobody ever would. It was just a thing I knew.

I set on the floor, quiet as could be, watching her big hands and her long fingers tracing the rough places and the eyelet cutouts in the pink fabric. Her lips moved at times, framing silent words I knew she would never say out loud.

I set in the sunshine on the floor and my eyes never left the sight of her while she put her words and thoughts through her finger tips into the work she was doing. She must have forgot I was there, for her stern, tired face relaxed, and her full, wide mouth softened. Her eyes glistened and rounded, and the green glass color of them lightened into a hazel color. The sun picked out their gold edged circles as I watched her touch the curtain and sort it into parts and cut it and remake it into something new.

After each piece was cut out, Mama smoothed it flat and rubbed her hands over it. She stretched some of the parts a few times, held them up to the light, and looked at each one awhile. Then she set to work again, her feet running in place, making the iron foot treadle fly on her old sewing machine.

I hoped someday she would look at me like that and touch me like she was touching that old pink lace curtain, but young as I was, I already knew that wasn't likely to happen, so I pretended I was the old pink lace curtain.

The dust motes floating in the sun filled air made my eyes water somethin' fierce, for they poured tears while I watched Mama working on that pink lace curtain.

Somehow Mama found a full slip to go under the dress she made from the pink lace curtain that day for Charlene to get married in.

Charlene came home in a few days and tried on the dress, and somethin' flashed between her and Mama for an instant. They looked at each other, and Charlene's mouth softened and trembled. Mama's eyes lightened again like they did while she was working on the pink lace curtain. The gold and green glass shine from Mama's eyes poured over Charlene like a dazzle bath. I saw it before they went back to their old ways, with Mama scolding and not touching Charlene.

Charlene took off again and didn't get married until a few years later. I never did know what happened to the pretty pink lace dress that Mama made from the curtain for her. I never remembered if she took it with her or not.

But after I watched Mama make Charlene's wedding dress from the pink lace curtain, I didn't mind the bare, ugly window in the living room without its pink curtain one bit. No, I never minded it at all.

17. Bennington and Belle

She saved up green stamps and then progressed to playing bingo while he was gone. Surprised, she kept winning. An idea formed in her mind. God must want her to get out of town too, because she kept on winning. She hid the money in a coffee can in the attic and bought a notebook and started writing in it. She hid that in the attic, too.

She moved up to playing black jack at the Elks Club and won again. She played the lottery a couple times, but no dice. Maybe God simply wanted her to win enough to buy a bus ticket out of town and have some cash to live on...

Short, frumpy, and portly in her well-worn best black dress, fake pearls at her throat, a shiny black patent leather goodwill purse hanging on her arm, she stood on the street corner nervously watching the traffic whiz by. Her short white hair peeked over the back collar of her ill-fitting black coat. The worn black shoes on her bunion-twisted, tired feet, hurt. She knew how she looked, but it was the best she could do. She clutched her purse closer. Evidently, the best she could do was enough. Luck stayed with her, and the small book she'd secretly written during the long hours he was gone, had sold this very day.

The title was "Lucky Gambler", in which she advanced theories on how to pick a winner when you are a loser. She was on the way home from the publisher's office with a small advance that would enable a one way fare aboard a bus out of town.

He'd be gone, as usual. She planned to grab her suitcase and leave the goodbye note she'd hid in her purse for some time now. She knew him. She wanted to leave without any sort of direct goodbye. She wanted to disappear out of his life, but she knew he would raise all kinds of holy hell and call the police and report her missing if she tried that. That man knew his luxuries, and intended on keeping them!

But right now, this instant, before anything else got done, she needed to focus on crossing the busy street in front of her. She studied the complexity of the wide, bustling street and the snarled, fast moving traffic with her usual timidity and dread.

That's when she noticed the man in front of the flower shop across the street. He was posing in front of a large copper bucket of orange tulips, and he was staring at her. Intently. Fiercely.

She drew her eyes away from him and edged towards the busy intersection. She waited to become scattered and ungrounded, drifting and floating like the little pieces of anonymous, aged paper that drifted into the area, only to be blown away by the hot drafts of rushing cars until they were torn and wordless, all ideas once written on them destroyed forever.

But it didn't happen. She frowned. She felt calm, like this was no big deal. What was the matter with her? She wondered if she accidentally took the wrong pill this morning. God knows there was enough of them to choose from! Maybe the strong pain pill she occasionally took for her back, that she knew was really for emotional pain and distress?

She frowned. Sometimes a scowl helped her master dread and trepidation with the serendipitous benefit of keeping other people from pushing at her with their darting eyes and impatient hands.

Five impossibly wide lanes to cross. Two wide lanes carrying traffic each way with a wide, efficient left turn lane in between them. She looked up at the red light riding high in the middle of the precise, indifferent four-way stop. "Stop! Go!" it shouted in colors without words.

It was an uncaring timer, an observer that couldn't and wouldn't cry in case of a mistake. It shone green yellow red, green yellow red turn only on arrow, high and mighty above it all, swinging impersonally between hard black wires attached to tall poles at the four corners of the busy intersection.

The city had painted wide white stripes at the edges of the left turn lane to warn the younger, faster drivers of the mostly new cars to slow down, to remind them there were other people sharing this world with them that didn't drive.

The city was known for its intelligence and its wealthy inhabitants, people who drove "Beamers", Jaguars, and Mercedes, racing around the city like fireflies on steroids. All the drivers, high and low, were impatient with the never ending lights and the bicycles and pedestrians.

She was familiar with the look that came over their faces when they saw her. Not many noticed her; but she knew exactly what those few were thinking. They believed walking was to gain torturous, sweat-free, talcum dampened exercise to tone their young, plump or toothpick-lean hard bodies. Or if done outdoors, to be seen and admired in the latest "togs" and shoes, with the latest step-counting, time-keeping, calorie-burning gizmos on their wrists.

None of them would ever walk for survival. The idea that someone would walk somewhere because they had to, dismayed them. Their carefully concealed contempt stayed plastered across their polite, self-absorbed faces as pity for those lost souls who'd never made it, who'd never reached the top, and for those who couldn't try anymore.

She watched them wrestle with their pity before they eased comfortably into the philosophy that migrants, old ladies, alcoholics, and lost young men and women were hopeless cases, stuck in inescapable patterns, while they themselves would never be there. It was left for someone else to handle, maybe even God; they'd heard God resided in the cities many shelters. Amen.

Others didn't bother thinking about it at all. Then the light changed, the moment was erased, and they rushed forward to a nowhere important enough to kill somebody over.

She'd graduated from the school of Hard Knocks. Earned a Masters in it. Working on a PHD in it. Menopause, and before that, child and husband rearing, always working to make ends meet. She'd led a thrifty life, giving up buying new clothes for herself and going to the second-hand stores for everything she needed. She'd worn old clothes with other women's secrets sewn into the seams while her husband and children wore new clothes and nice shoes. The children were proud of themselves. They preened in front of her, soliciting compliments. They were socially adept and didn't understand why she didn't want to leave the house much. They scolded her while she stood in front of the bathroom mirror, cutting her hair and giving herself home perms to save money to spend on them.

They grew further away. She aged and grew more inward. Her husband died and her children left her far behind while her body changed and drove her crazy. She gained weight and her shoe size grew, and gave her bunions and the times that could have been, vanished forever.

A small town girl, she'd led a small town life, expecting to die of old age in the same town. Until she met a guy at a senior dance. He bragged about being from a big city. On impulse, she ran away with him and now she was living with him in that big city.

It should have been easier, but it wasn't. He was an old man who thought he was a spring chicken because he was two years younger than her. He called her his "partner" and stared at twenty seven year old girls.

He'd proposed. She'd said no. She'd turned for solace to her favorite old movies. She cleaned his nasty house and painted with Errol Flynn working beside her. She polished and scrubbed with Gary Cooper organizing things. She raked and burned and carried out trash with Spencer Tracy and Humphrey Bogart helping her.

She worked for months in his dirty, gloomy house while he left her to go drink, eat, and smoke pot with his friends.

"Good riddance!" she thought. John Wayne nodded in agreement.

He resented her efforts, then took credit for everything she improved, leaving her silent black and white movie star companions aghast and appalled. John Wayne said to take the bus out of town like Marilyn Monroe did in Bus Stop.

"Move on, Pilgrim." he told her.

Lately, the man sensed something was wrong, and he vaguely saw the error of his ways. He changed some. She could see the effort it cost him, and knew it was temporary. He gave her a few grudging compliments, and even did the cooking sometimes but never the dishes. Marlon Brando helped her with those. He came home at a decent hour some nights, at least more often than usual, to let her know she'd finally earned his love while he followed her around, asking for bedroom time or when dinner would be ready. Clark Kent asked her if he could take him out back and beat the crap out of him. She said maybe soon.

Ward Bond, Burt Lancaster, Cary Grant and the rest all agreed that she'd got herself into another fix. No money. Lonely and on foot without a car. She was from a small, flat town far away from this big hilly, wet city that smelled like fish.

It was time to figure out ways to make money so she could leave the dank city and him, far behind. Loretta Young suggested learning card games. She practiced while Gary Cooper watched and Willie Mosconi advised.

Orson Welles and Somerset Maugham edited the book. It didn't take them long, but they owed a favor to Marlon. Of course, it sold. The odds were heavily in their favor.

The light changed. She stepped down from the curb, and started across the street.

She glanced across the street. The man in front of the flower shop was still watching her. The crosswalk led straight across the street to him. She kept walking. She had to; it was the only way to get across the street.

The man was handsome, aged, and proud. He exuded an air of confidence and the sophistication of a leading man in her beloved black and white movies. A part of her tried to make him absurd, to not believe any man would be dressed as he was in the middle of the day in real life, but she simply wondered what his name was.

He was short and rather slender. He wore a tuxedo with a pink carnation in his lapel. His black shoes were shiny, his tuxedo fit him perfectly, and his wavy white hair framed a strong, tanned face that put her in mind of Don Ameche.

He stared at her. She wondered if something was wrong with her dress or her short, fine hair. She heard Elizabeth Taylor accusing her in a little voice of letting her hair turn mostly dull gray, of cutting it short and not perming it and of never wearing makeup any more.

She touched her hair and ran her hand down

her open coat and dress to make sure she was decent, that her slip wasn't showing, that she hadn't caught the edge of her dress in her purse, accidentally showing off her underwear like she did once back in seventh grade.

Everything seemed to be in its proper place. Maybe the man was mistaking her for someone else. She didn't noticed the florist that stepped out of the flower shop to wave at someone at the café across the street. She didn't notice that he waved back; that they both turned and fastened their eyes on her. In an instant, the flutter of wings sang through the air. John Wayne and Tom Mix chuckled. Charlie Chaplin laughed out loud.

A sudden thought flashed through her mind. No, she couldn't. She wouldn't. She was a fool! She'd been wrong too many times to ever try again. But Tallulah whispered in her ear and Carol tugged at her arm. Spencer hummed. Bogie snarled. She gave in. They must know what they were doing. They always did. She trusted them.

Scenes from her favorite, beloved, old black and white romance movies flooded her mind. She pictured her and the man across the street playing out their favorite parts together. For a long moment in time, she became Ginger Rogers to the man's Fred Astaire; Lauren Bacall to his Humphrey Bogart. Gene Kelly danced by her side and she was the love of Clark Gable's life.

She felt the precious alchemy of Beauty run through her. Frumpy, cracked, and dry fell away. Youth returned, with all its gorgeous hormones and rhythms. She stood straight and proud. Age didn't matter anymore. She fluffed her silver hair, smoothed the bosomy front of her dress, and patted her purse with the book advance in it.

For the first time in her life, she absolutely knew someone saw her as a thoroughly beautiful woman. At last! She wasn't religious or even devout, but she knew they saw what the angels saw in her. What angels? She didn't know. Just that they were suddenly there. Joy spread through her in exotic, tantalizing colors and scents. She'd starved all her life, waiting for someone, anyone, to see who she was, to applaud her ageless, dancing soul. That's all she'd ever needed to get through her absurd, mistake riddled life.

She realized without regret that she would no longer be able to sacrifice herself for anyone else; she couldn't give herself away to their causes and more. That was over and done with.

She had a book deal, thanks to Orson and Bill and the others, and money in her purse and a lovely man staring at her like she was a real honey. Yes. At last her life belonged to her, for better or worse.

Cary Grant said, "Let's move on; having an epiphany while crossing a busy street is not the safest thing to do." Spencer took her arm and propelled her forward. She clutched her purse tight as she moved steadily towards the man who bore a striking resemblance to Errol Flynn. No, maybe Ronald Coleman.

÷

Twill Bennington missed his wife furiously every second the first year after she passed. The second year, he began to accept a few things about his new life without her. But he knew he would never like living alone. There was no one to watch his beloved black and white movies with him except Butch, his beloved boxer. A few years went by, and Butch died, too. Now there was nobody.

There was nothing left to live for, except his beloved movies of Talullah, Ida, and Claudette. Then the time came when even they could not hold him here any longer. It was time for him to go. He would figure out how to do it tomorrow.

He went to bed and fell into a dream. A voice that sounded a bit like Sterling Holloway's informed him that he was owed one by somebody upstairs for whatever reason, so they were sending Burt and Roz, a team of angelic matchmakers who didn't make too many mistakes, to help him. He would have to stay alive. He began to dream deeper. Someone chuckled at his snores.

÷

Following instructions he wasn't consciously aware of, Twill took his tuxedo to the cleaners the next morning instead of purchasing a noose at the hardware store. Then he went home and polished his shoes, after which he went back out and bought new black socks, half dozen pair of luridly patterned boxer shorts, and white all cotton under shirts. He carried them home and packed them into his worn suitcase.

Well, he had to have a new white shirt, so he bought a pink carnation from the florist on the corner who looked like an angel with wings at the oddest times on his way to the Smith Brothers clothing store. It was the first flower he'd bought since Thelma and Butch passed away. He placed the carnation in the lapel of his suit coat.

Sure, there was plenty of money to spend on things, but there was nothing he'd wanted until now. He bought his shirt, picked up his tux from the cleaners, took it home and hung it in the closet.

He woke up the next morning, ate his breakfast, and gave notice to the paper boy. At one o'clock, he called and hired a real estate company to take care of his house for awhile. He guessed he was going on a trip, though he didn't know where to yet.

Now here he stood, suitcase by his side, standing on a busy street corner, yearning to dance with a woman crossing the street who looked like Myrna Loy one minute and Betty Davis the next.

Twill was a sensible, practical man who was now thoroughly mystified at what he was up to. He looked around. He wondered what was happening to him. He was old, and he didn't want to get locked up. He glanced at the man drinking coffee at an outside table at the cafe across the street. The man nodded and smiled at him. Suddenly Twill felt an angel's wing brush his shoulder. His worry dropped away. Suddenly he felt supremely confident that he was exactly where he needed to be, whether he understood it or not. He was glad he'd changed his mind about going to the hardware store.

Time passed in slow motion. Agnes Belle saw her reflection shining in the man's eyes. She stepped up on the curb and stood there, swaying like a newly-bloomed spring daffodil dressed in yellow, just like Greta Garbo did in one of her movies.

The handsome stranger in front of her tilted his head to one side and threw his arms out, palms up, in a universal gesture that said it doesn't get any better than this! Just like Eric Hamsomer did in his famous movie, "Love Happened at the Ritz." They never noticed the smiling people flowing past and around them.

Twill Bennington smiled at the beautiful woman standing in front of him. There was a hint of Joan Blondell about her. He removed his hat and bowed to her.

"Would you join me for a cup of coffee?" he asked politely.

She nodded and smiled at the dapper man wearing a tuxedo with a pink carnation in his lapel in the middle of the day. He looked a bit like Charles Boyer. Somehow he grew a bit taller, younger, and even more handsome. Twill touched his black Fedora to his heart, looked deep into her eyes and murmured something.

Agnes tried to read his lips; the noise of the traffic always made her turn off her hearing aids. They moved to an outside table at the diner next to the florists shop so they could hear each other. Two hours later, they rose from the table, smiling at each other.

"I shall call you Belle." He announced, taking her arm.

"Yes." she answered. "Belle and Bennington on a mission!"

'Yes!" he agreed. They strolled down the street shoulder to shoulder with Twill carrying his suitcase.

The man sitting at the café across the street watched closely as the drab old couple dressed in black and white and gray slowly make their way out of sight.

Though he'd seen it time and again in both the aged and the young, Burt never grew tired of watching love meet its match. Matchmaking was an ageless art he was adept at, actually an expert; he'd become one over eons of time.

He glanced across the street at the lovely angel in the florist shop, his sidekick Roz. She was the other half of their angel team. They worked for the Division of Angelic Activities; Romance Department, Cloud Number Four, Matchmakers For Forgotten Old Souls. Matchmaking was their specialty; they'd done it again.

Their thorough research had paid off once again. The file from their research department said Agnes Belle looked sort of like Twill's deceased wife of many years; they'd danced to Ginger and Fred and watched old black and white movies together countless times.

Burt and Roz checked his vitals and heart carefully to make sure there was still room in it for a new love, one who was short with a tendency to make mistakes, before they began their mission.

Roz watched them leave through the window of the flower shop. The old couple were now gifted with late blooming luck and love. Twill Bennington was definitely hell bent on rescuing Agnes Belle. She watched until they were out of sight before she sighed sentimentally sending the man across the street a quick, longing glance.

He fixed his gaze on Roz. She smiled at him. He watched the sun glinting off her white wings as they fluttered. He sighed with adoration, picked up his coffee cup and took a sip. Sometimes it was well worth being a mature romance angel well versed in helping the countless older shades of love to bloom again. Turning them into romances took fine tuning and teamwork. He cast another admiring glance across the street.

÷

Twill and Belle headed to the man's house to sneakily snatch away her runaway suitcase, packed and hidden under a burlap sack in a back corner of the ancient shed behind the house. How easy it was to squirrel it away while the man sat inside in his recliner, stoned and watching sports! They slipped in the back gate, retrieved the suitcase; Twill waited, holding her suitcase while she slipped into the attic to retrieve the can of money.

÷

The old couple climbed the bus steps carrying a stack of old movie magazines, two bags of popcorn, sodas, and two worn suitcases. They settled into their seats as the bus doors closed. They left the bus stop for parts unknown, just like Marilyn and Hope Lange, Don Murray, and a slew of others did in the past. Across from them sat John Wayne. Behind them sat Montgomery Clift and Tallulah Bankhead. Belle and Bennington smiled happily at them and offered them popcorn.

18. Kate Osgood's Odes to a Few Old Boyfriends

Well, there I stood, a' hangin' on to that worn out suitcase like a damn burr stuck to a mothball frayed fringe, with no damn cat around to knock it loose. Yep. I was lost in the damn woods again, with wolves around me just like Little Red Riding Hood, only I'm just a southern gal with a suitcase full of old notes, old love letters and what have ye'! Well, there's stuff in it about woods and other things, in case you git' lost sometime too, like little Red Riding Hood.

They say when lightning strikes a tree, it makes the sap inside the tree boil, and that's why the tree explodes. That could be a shiner story. They'll say anything, ya' know.

There's tall, dark and handsome in pictures in there, too. There's short and cute with flashing white teeth and dimples. Then there's the rest of us usual folks just a' smilin' away.

In my life there's been books, sling shots, bicycles, rainy days, corn on the cob and warm red tomatoes stole from the garden early in the mornin' or at noon when nobody's lookin'.

Southern mountain women like me know it is advisable to have a goodly amount of grit in yer' craw before ya' set about findin' a man fer' yerself'.

Tin cans
Stone crocks
Bony, clingy toes
Available for Parts and labor
Crick rocks

Dear Sweeney Scott Upton,

That old three story red brick school standin' in the middle of town got tore down years ago. You took a' hold of my heart back then in seventh grade, and it is still in your hands, though I may have had a few flings along the way, mainly cause' you're not around.

Seems like I met you yesterday when we spent fall days and red and gold leaves with us a' holdin' hands, and you a' drawin' me up close when the wind blowed cold, predictin' a long winter ahead.

The first time I seen you was at the noon dance in the gym. Me short and thin as a year old dogwood sapling, and you tall and blond as a growin' copper beech. I was shy as a doe. I hid behind the girls lined up on one side of the gym in their ponytails, pageboys, and poodle skirts.

The girls swayed like bouquets of forget-me-nots waitin' for the boys to cross the floor to ask them to dance. I tried to stay hid, but I loved the music and dancin' so much I always ended up out front.

The boys wore crew cuts cut so close the shapes and bumps on their heads showed, and starched, short sleeve plaid shirts and ironed kakis with sharp creases. They lined up on the other side of the gym like soldiers in uniforms, which some of you later became, to the woe of us women you left behind.

I remember the "Sadie Hawkins" dances when the girls in the poodle skirts and neck scarves got to ask the boys to dance, and how you boys acted like you really didn't give a damn if you got asked or not.

I remember Palmer Lowe and all them older bad boys in their black leather jackets, tight jeans, and white t-shirts with packs of cigarettes rolled up in their sleeves. Big silver butane lighters outlined their pockets. They kept small black combs in their watch pockets and they could whip them out faster than a cowboy holding a loaded gun in a popular weekly western. They kept their hair loaded with Brylcreem and combed up into high rolls.

They bunched up in a corner of the gym, waiting out the noon dances. The dances were their penance for always being in trouble. The teachers thought if they went to the noon dances, they'd learn from the rest of us how to behave.

I rushed outside after school right along with a bunch of other girls to watch them leave on their motorcycles before the bus come to pick up us ordinary kids. They left noisy clouds of spent motorcycle gas hangin' in the air but a strong wind never moved a hair on a single head of em'.

You were tall, blond, smart as a whip, a golden, handsome boy, full of a good future, an only child. You watched me from across the gym. You stood with the rich kids, and I didn't miss for one second how those girls looked at you.

I was poor as a church mouse and didn't know one thing about clothes or good manners or anything else. But I knew how to spell real good, always did. Even when I barely got enough food to stay alive and no winter coat. I only knew how to survive in the life I lived.

I remember our first dance. You crossed the gym floor to me and I didn't chicken out and hide like I always did whenever I saw you comin'.

My first dance with a boy. You shook like a leaf in a high gale while we danced. You looked down at me. "When we grow up, I'm going to marry you."

Well, it was all over right then, during that first slow dance. My heart fell right into your chest where yours was a' waitin', and I nodded yes. Yep. I fell into your chest, and almost into your heart. Almost. I got mighty close. I didn't know it back then, but it was already too late for me concerning men.

Those jealous girls who wanted to go steady with you and your friends made it hard for us, but they never scared me off. I did. I quit you, not due to lack of love, but due to being scared, and I broke both our hearts.

Well, school went on clear through graduation with us apart. Then you got called up to go to Viet Nam.

We stayed apart until you come home on leave. I'd moved to town and got a job, and you found me reading at the library on a Saturday morning. You looked so good in your soldier's uniform. You'd filled out, and I felt your quiet authority. You knew who you were in the world, which was more than I could ever say about myself.

We walked and talked and held hands and looked at our reflections in the store windows of that small town like we did back in seventh grade. We went to Louie's Dairy Bar and ordered cherry cokes and you looked at me the way you always did, like I was divine, and I looked at you like that too, and we held hands and danced a little bit on the sidewalk in the orange and red autumn leaves.

But divination runs in my mean, mostly crazy family, and I trembled like it was winter as I promised you I would stop running and wait for you to come home. You left, and in no time, the news flew back, along with a closed casket and a black bracelet.

I couldn't stand it no more, so I moved away. I never went back. Except once. I went back once on a visit to our small town many years later. The school and the stores we once knew were gone. I was sitting in a chain restaurant visiting with a girl we went to school with. We were talking about old times when your name came up. She said there was something she'd forgot to tell me way back then.

"Remember when I worked in the dairy bar?"

I nodded yes.

"Well, Sweeney Scott Upton came in looking for you. He said he was home on a two day leave, and he needed to find you as fast as he could. He wrote something down on a piece of paper before he left. He asked me to give it to you, but it slipped my mind, then I lost the paper. You know, I forgot all about it until just now. Isn't it sad he didn't have more time at home before he went back over there and stepped on a land mine carrying a wounded guy to a helicopter?"

I will hate her forever for the time she stole away from us.

So, Sweeney Scott Upton, I stand at your grave in our little town cemetery for the first time. Your beautiful life brought me back here. You will always be a shining light in my life. Through my memories you will always live.

When each seventeen September rolls around, I recall the coldness of that long night when I put out the candles for you and me and cried out cracked and resistant prayers of entreaty. I didn't know any better back then than to believe that we could hoard time in the miser's cupboard and take it out and use it as we pleased.

Today I stand here, holdin' a yellowed paper of explanation, wearin' a worn black metal bracelet with your name on it, finally accepting the Book of Revelations laying at my feet. It's chased me a long time, so I came back here to claim it, and lay it to rest.

Now my love, sweet dreams and blessed rest, lay your head upon my breast and I will hold you gently and for always. I will wear blue for you again and sit on the new grass in the springtime where the old school stood and I will count the days and name the flowers growing there for you.

Sometimes your wide smile filled with humor reaches out to me when I see something funny I know you would've liked. I yearn to rest my head against your heart like I did the first time we danced. I remember how well it fit there when we were young and took for granted that life was going to go on forever.

Maybe someday I'll come back again to our small town that's grown so big nobody knows each other anymore, and place purple flowers where you rest, and recount the memories we share, the ones stored in my heart. And I will tell you more about my kids and their kids and about being a grandmother. Odds are against it, though. But hope never ends.

Signed your true love,
Ester Phellps

Here's one that fled under the bridge.
Maybe he escaped from a fate worse
than death. Maybe we both did.

Tombstone Territory

Granite
Marble

Daniel David Gridstone

First time I seen you was in church in the springtime. You were an older man of sixteen. I was mesmerized, like a lost soul dazed and wanderin' home from seein' a copperhead on the road.

I set right down behind you to get my eyes full. I got busy memorizing your straight brown hair and the curve of your neck. I decided you were just tall enough so the top of my head would fit neat right under your chin.

You didn't pay me one minute's attention until me and my sister stood by the piano in the front of the church and sung that duet when we turned fourteen. Her soprano and me alto.

Sunday mornin' light shined through the stained glass window behind us, highlightin' our new washed hair and new matchin' homemade lavender sprigged blouses and skirts. Slim and pretty as dolls we was, and we knew it, and took great pleasure in it.

Your brown eyes sparkled and you said, "Hi," to me and strolled on past to your old black car that day. Right that minute, I thought it was too bad you was old enough to drive. I studied on it, and knew you was mine, even though I could see you was made of oak and iron water that generally whiles itself along the wrong path of a troublesome creek.

After a time of worry caused by you not making up your mind which creek bed to foller', the old black dial phone rung for me every Wednesday night. We worded our way along, never naming our home troubles or who we was to each other, for we didn't know any of that mattered back then.

Friday and Saturday nights you picked me up in your black 39' Coupe, and we escaped out to the blacktopped highway. The smell of warm summer dust and the growin' crops in the fields set us free. I scooted right up tight against you and fell into your aftershave while we hummed songs on the radio.

We closed our enemies out. It was just you and me. Once you drove us to an amusement park in another state. I got scared and clung to you on the roller coaster while you laughed. You held my hand at drive-in movies and bought us hamburgers. We set together in church on Sundays, singin' and holdin' hands.

I wore your high school ring on a chain around my neck that summer and clear into fall. It was the same as a wedding ring to me. Oh, that was a good time!

÷

School started, then come the bad time, all because of you! I'll never forget standin' upstairs in the church loft, not knowin' what was a' comin'. Not ready. Never. You took me to a place where I couldn't see your face to ask for your ring back so you could date a new girl in your school. Blabbermouth. Blab. Blab. Blab. Dinah, you said her name was. You said she was tall and blond with fancy clothes like Dinah Shore. And you were on the football team and student council. You said the two of you belonged together, and I didn't even go to your school.

November seventh, many years ago, at seven thirty four p.m. high up in a darkened church loft, my heart got broke. You damn meanie! You just had to go do it in a church and pull God into the act, which made it worse, 'cause God, at that time in my life was a grumpy old male settin' somewhere off on a throne who liked revenge a whole bunch!

I don't remember how I got home.

I think you may have taken me home.

I don't know.

My world ended, at least until the next spring. I'd never thought past you and me. I lost my mind, and my soul wandered off for a long time. I never remembered the next months in my life, not ever again. I still can't recall anything except wandering through Tombstone Territory, cold as a granite stone, searchin' for my name on one.

Then spring showed up again and I discovered I wasn't dead from the grief you put me through. One morning I come back from wherever I'd been. I found myself standing in my father's garden, staring at the blue morning glories winding their way through young tomato plants, greenly hopeful of a full life ahead. I studied them. They were going for it! Well, what the hell, I would go for it, too. So life went on.

The summers flew by, and with them came my kids and all kinds of different kinds of love to learn. I moved across the country while you stayed stuck in your little town where you got to be a big fish in a little pond. You married and had two kids, a boy and a girl. So did I.

I was setting with my first grandchild on my lap when we spoke again. I told you how you broke my heart way back then, and what a cad you were. You said we were just kids. I said that didn't make any difference. I said I'd stayed a southern woman with a suitcase ever since, and you best give me give me that apology now.

Well, we mailed each other letters and cards at Christmas and birthdays and once in a while in between. You said to send yours to a post office box cause' your wife didn't like you having women friends. I didn't like it, but I went along with you. I sent you my new address each time I moved. When winter set in each year, I sometimes wondered what a good, warm blanket you might have made.

Everything went along fine until you started callin' me up instead of writin'. I didn't mind cheering you up. You said I made you laugh. Well, then I let you keep a' callin' cause' your ex-wife and your wife started dyin' off at the same time. I listened steady to all that misery you were going through. Then they died off within three months of each other, and you went nuts and blamed me. Said I was the other woman! Stupid idiot! All over a few letters and cards in which I didn't write anything but daily news! Well, there were the phone calls. But they didn't amount to a hill of beans. They were grief calls, fool!

Then you called and wanted to come and get me and take me back home with you, like I was a soft, old chair, to take care of your hurt and madness over losing them!

Hello! Duh!

I wouldn't go or take the blame, 'cause there was never any for me to take, buddy boy! Never was! Takin' your wives from you was God's work, not mine!

I wouldn't do it, and you wouldn't wait for me to figure out what else we could do, so you did just exactly what you did to me before. You grabbed another woman quick, Mr. Big Shot, before either of the ones who'd put up with your bad temper was even cold in the ground. I haven't heard hide nor hair out of you since, and damn good riddance!

I want you to know, you piss ant jerk, that I burned the letters and cards and didn't mourn for you one minute like I did when I was young. I went on with my life, just like I was forced to do before because of you, only this time, it was good riddance to you!

Signed by Gladys Touget Ridayu. Ha ha!

Hattie McDuff was never a good man picker. While she was living with a monster, she come across a lonesome, handsome cowboy and fell for him like a ton of bricks flattening a house of cards.

Well, she learned from him that there's Pintos and quarter horses and wranglers and geldings and studs and bunkhouses and saddles and coyotes and cattle. Dust and ropes and buckboards. Women and fillies and bars. Take yer' pick. Just like in the western movies.

Lucky West Wellborn

Here's how the black and white movie started...

He's leaning up against the fender of his car, waiting for her, hours before them, maybe dinner and a movie. She's sitting with friends, laughing and talking in a jumble of moving boxes. He intends to ask her out.

Her ex told him she was moving. He wanted to know where to. But he didn't ask the ex. He almost called her, but he drove over to her place instead.

One of her friends answered the door. Judy Garland, he thought she said her name was. He followed her into the little apartment in the back of the house. He stopped in the doorway as Judy, maybe that was her name, introduced him to, was it Grace Kelly and Jean Harlow, and Marion Davies?

They were all sitting around on the floor and on a couple of orange crates, taking a break, eating takeout pizza. There was no furniture or a bed or much of anything left because the ex stole everything including her underwear, for he was a predator. The ex always was one, a hidden sneak who worked steadily on plans to take away all her tomorrows without him being blamed. She kicked him out. He stole everything she owned one day while she was at work and their little girl was at the babysitter's. He threatened her life and harassed her constantly, but her humor never left, and neither did her girlfriends.

They rallied together and gave her a couple cats, an old sofa, and new underwear. Now they were helping her move into the tiny apartment in the back of the house. She planned to live there with her precious daughter and rent out the front to keep the mortgage paid.

The girls, maybe Mary Pickford and Shelley Duvall?- all stopped talking and watched her stunned disbelief and delight at seeing him standing in the doorway. They watched him gaze at her as though they didn't exist. Well, how about that? He announced to her only-in front of them, that today was his birthday, and what he wanted most of all was for her to go out with him tonight.

Jenny Lind, Mary Astor, and Amelia Earhart, whatever their names were, giggled. He ignored them with his usual elegance, grace, and good looks. She walked over to him. She looked up into his eyes and said, "Yes, I would love to, but you're going to have to give me time to get ready."

Well, that all sounds romantic enough with a potentially good ending, but let's not forget about the ex-husband, the Monster she needed help to battle.

She told him about the monster. He said he didn't believe it; the Monster was no Monster. Lucky, bless his lonesome cowboy heart, shied away from the terrible part of her life. Her heart broke. She'd loved Lonesome Lucky from afar too long.

She waited for him to change his mind. He went away, and after three weeks of waiting for his call, the phone rang. He said he was with some little gals at a party and he would probably spend the night there. He'd call her tomorrow. Well, that did it. It may have been the era of free love and foolin' around with everybody for him, but not for her! She was a one woman man, now kicked to the curb.

She turned to survival instead of him. Every step she took away from that phone call cut away at the blood and bone of her for she loved Lucky West Wellborn beyond himself. Which meant that he was her Clark Gable, her Tyrone Power, her Hop Along Cassidy.

She turned the TV off and kept on going. They had to survive the Monster. Well, maybe there would be time for true love later.

She grabbed another man who protected her and her girl from the Monster. They survived, lived, and thrived, haphazard and half assed until that marriage broke up a few years later.

Well, that old cowboy Lucky still calls her once in awhile. He don't know why, but she does. She notes the lilt in his voice that once charmed the pants off of any woman. Maybe it still did. She never asks.

He tells her she was beautiful back then and marvels at Greta Garbo's mystery and thinness. He remembers Hedy Lamarr, Jane Russel, and Joan Fontaine. He never mentions her cousin Pam or friends Janie and Sharon, or her daughter's name, and never the loss he forced her to take back then to survive, to overcome a Monster.

She stands in her kitchen, years away from those days, in a thin and old pink robe, made for her by a girlfriend who sewed her name in scrolls across the top left side of it. She smoothes her hand across the worn threads of the name.

As she listens, she tugs the robe tighter around herself to protect stretch marks and a large belly from his words. She pulls the robe collar higher to hide the wrinkles in the back of her neck.

He wanted a woman littler than him and she was always bigger than him except for a short time way back then. She'd known that for awhile. What could have been sometimes dies a slow, damn death. She laughs and says once more, "I'll never be twenty two again. Don't wanna' be. Well, nice hearing from you. Take good care of yourself, and call again sometime."

Sebastian B.(B. for bastard) Jockmore

He's made of Brass
Bronze
Night shades
And one sorry ass!

We rode up through the hills with Sebastian sneaking sideways glances at the wrinkles around my wrists leading down to the hundreds of fine lines ending at my knuckles. He studied the road signs, tall and lanky and tan and bland, to keep from looking at the lines in my face. He was afraid my eyes would catch his, and I would know what he was up to. I am seven years older than him, and he just can't stand it.

He just terminated a three month affair with a twenty one year old who got pregnant and he had to pay for the abortion. He wondered why she cried when he told her he didn't love her and never did, he was only on the rebound from someone who'd broke his heart, and he was sorry, but she could understand, couldn't she?

He was kind enough not to mention to her that the girl he was chasing when he wasn't with her was twenty-two, and he was leaving desperate notes under the wipers of her old car every time he got back from one of his business trips during which he spent big bucks picking up women in bars or on call girls.

He whined to them about the hard time he was having without his girlfriend and her three children who'd lived with him for the past three, no, maybe it was five years now, then she left him for no reason. Unless you included his faithlessness which he said he couldn't help, which he confessed to her whenever he couldn't take the pressure of cheating any more, but no more than fifteen times.

He drove higher up into the hills still talking about his numbered troubles, while I rode silently in the passenger seat, with Arthur, his sidekick riding in the back seat, both of us listening while the numbers mounted up.

That was before we both left him, my beloved Arthur to cancer, too late for me to discover more of the beauty of him, and me to a little house near the ocean, where old age isn't so hard to face anymore. Better than listening to that bastard Sebastian.

Yep. I missed out on Arthur because I was busy looking at that bastard Sebastian. That's me back then. Not now when it's too late.

Oh well.
Here's the moral of this story.

Try to remember Arthur when you're out roaming the woods like little Red Riding Hood with your suitcase in your hand. If you can't find your Arthur, just slap another sticker on that worn out suitcase, heft yer' gizzies, and get the hell out of the woods!

Signed, Elzabeth Watson Frymore

About the Author

Patsy Stanley is an artist, illustrator, author and nature advocate. She has authored and illustrated both nonfiction and fiction books including romance novels, children's books, energy books and art books. She can reached at patsystanley123@gmail.com for questions or comments.

Books by Patsy Stanley:

Metaphysical books:
Chakras, Meridians and the Color Energies
The Spiritual Nature of Atomic Structure
The Use of Shield Energies
The Elements
Sound Energies
The Mental Body

Novels:
Addition Jones
Emerald Hawk's Flight
Avalon Blue's Quest

A Collection of Short stories- An Older Wine

Books authored and illustrated by Patsy Stanley:
Suitable for Children and all young at heart readers.
Christmas Stories From the Crone's Castle
The Dreadful Noises of Landoshar

Big Al's Christmas Wedding

Native American:
The Green Mountain Shaman
Red Leaf

The first three novels in my new
Desert Oasis Series are now available!

Cowboy Johnson's Desert Oasis
Mama and the 57' Mercury

Fleeing a desperate situation in her 57' Merc', Mama and daughter Geena head south to try to start a new life. In a desert in New Mexico, they stop at a gas station and grocery store, formerly a little white church. Parked in a 59' pink Cadillac convertible at the side of the store under the only shade tree for miles sits a woman crying loud enough to break the sound barrier. The store owner, the mysterious Cowboy Johnson, steps out and urges them to help her. Mama and Geena, both being psychics who specialize in appreciating land yachts, are hooked.

The adventures begin in book one with the gradual gathering of a group of lost, hiding out, secret laden, mostly psychic misfits moving into the store. When the store is full and running over with misfits, isolates and hermits, in self defense, William and Cowboy Johnson build a motel, restaurant, and gift shop. They name it Cowboy Johnson's Desert Oasis.

The misfits build a life together, then move on

to new lives, one after the other as time passes. But they return to the store each year for Christmas, back to the roots they grew together to celebrate and strengthen each other for the new year ahead. An old fashioned read, one to be savored like a piece of hot chocolate cake, a story from an era of time rich in two lane blacktopped roads, land yachts, and the many endless roads leading to love.

Book Two

The Red Cactus Desert
Geena and the 59' Dodge Lancer

Twelve year old Geena escapes the clutches of her Shadow-tainted father and the town that supports him. Fleeing south with Mama in a 57' Mercury, they stop at a desert store in New Mexico. Having inherited the Sight from Mama, she immediately knows the store is her new home, and Cowboy Johnson, the owner, the good father she needs. Now she has protection and a family — and love at first sight — when she meets Ray Makepeace. More misfits settle into the store. But families carry both strengths and weaknesses and the misfits have plenty of both.

Geena and Ray's love is in for a bumpy ride. Normaine won't marry beautiful, dapper Eddy. Mama is terrified of returning Cowboy Johnson's steadfast, calm love. William the Dude

236

Makepeace makes troubling decisions based on his arthritis.

Still, love will have its way, traveling the many paths it takes to stay true to the soul each misfit carries. Interspersed here and there are ©children's stories the author is currently making into children's books. Geena's coming of age story is an inspiring tale of innocence and courage.

Book Three

The Three Cactus Limbo
Bud's Garage and the Quest of the Three Magi

Bud Spinner, a fear-filled reclusive garage owner, a shy inner-knower of hidden goodness in people, helps Map Girl and Geena escape Ardenville with cash and a map. Bud secretly writes car fix-it manuals, banking the money in another town. Bud, Ben, and Andy, two other fear-filled recluses in town, find each other and become fast friends. Bud repairs cars. Ben reads science fiction. Andy fishes unsuccessfully.

Unknown to themselves as well as the town, they are able to detect good and evil, the hidden emotions and intentions in others. Constantly overwhelmed by their secret, hidden gifts, they stay extremely resistant to the ills of the outside world. Their solution is to hide.

Easily overwhelmed by nature and the unknown as well as people, they buy a cabin and spend weekends away from Ardenville. But Dan, a private eye hired by Mama to keep tabs on her ex, ejects them from their cabin, forcing them to flee Ardenville. They start out on their first road trip, carrying a gift for Map Girl. After visiting Map Girl, Miss Emma, a world famous artist, and her father, William the Dude Makepeace, talk them into staying at a remote monastery for awhile. They plan to spend Christmas with Map Girl, not knowing the unexpected ways of Fate will step in again to change everything.

Book Four
Away in a Desert
Susan Sugar Diamond

Is in the works!

* 9 7 8 1 7 3 2 8 5 5 2 5 0 *